**She wasn't at al~~~~~
Cameron~~~~~**

They'd worked as a team today at the soup kitchen. It gave her a new insight into the fire chief. Most men would have bolted after a woman's rejection of a date.

She studied him for a moment. Cameron wasn't just trying to get to know her. She'd seen him talking, then praying with a couple of people after the meal began. Many of them knew him and called him Chief Cam.

Just who was Cameron Jackson?

"I'm going to let Pastor Hines know that the soup kitchen needs some volunteers," Cameron said.

"I'm just glad you and your friends came to the rescue. Thank you."

At some point during the meal service, Summer had decided that a date with a man who would give the homeless almost seven hours of his day was a date she'd like to go on.

Summer let Cameron escort her out the back door and toward her car in the parking lot.

"If the offer is still open," she said, "I'd like to have dinner with you."

Books by Felicia Mason

Love Inspired

Sweet Accord
Sweet Harmony
Gabriel's Discovery
The Fireman Finds a Wife

Love Inspired Single Title

Sweet Devotion

FELICIA MASON

is a journalist who writes fiction in her free time. Her Love Inspired Suspense novel *Gabriel's Discovery* was a finalist for the 2005 RITA® Award from Romance Writers of America. She has been a college professor, a Sunday school teacher and a member of several choirs. When she is not writing, she enjoys reading, traveling to new places, scrapbooking and quilting. She resides in Virginia.

The Fireman Finds a Wife

Felicia Mason

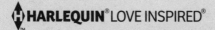

Recycling programs
for this product may
not exist in your area.

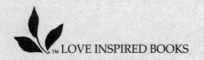

™ LOVE INSPIRED BOOKS

ISBN-13: 978-0-373-81766-5

THE FIREMAN FINDS A WIFE

Copyright © 2014 by Felicia Mason

www.Harlequin.com

Printed in U.S.A.

When you pass through the waters, I will be with you; and when you pass through the rivers, they will not sweep over you. When you walk through the fire, you will not be burned; the flames will not set you ablaze. Do not be afraid, for I am with you.

—*Isaiah* 43:2–5

For Pastor Matt Sabo,
who took a photograph of three ministers and
provided the connecting thread that would bring
together an idea that had been brewing with me
for many years. Thanks, Matt, for prompting the
idea for the Common Ground ministry that would
connect three diverse fictional congregations.

Acknowledgments

A thank you to Melissa Endlich at
Harlequin Enterprises, who welcomed me back into
the Love Inspired family after an extended hiatus.

Chapter One

"I'm glad you made me do this," Summer Spencer said.

Her older sister gave her an odd look as she sliced a sliver of cheesecake from the small wedge on her plate.

"Cheesecake, especially your raspberry cheesecake, is always a good idea," Spring said.

The sisters were taking a break in the sunroom off Summer's large, light-filled gourmet kitchen. Smiling, Summer put her own fork down, rested her elbows on the table and her chin in her hands.

"Not this," she said, clarifying with a nod toward the table. "I'm glad you made me come home to Cedar Springs. This was a good move for me. The only downside has been dealing with Ilsa Keller at Manna. I volunteered at the church's soup kitchen to help people, not to be in a constant turf battle with her."

"Ilsa can be…" Spring paused, looking for the right word. "Territorial."

Summer grimaced. "Dictatorial is the word I'd use."

With a nod, her sister conceded the point. "She means well."

"We're already shorthanded," Summer said. "And three more volunteers have quit. One came to me in tears asking if I could do something, and another stormed out the back door five minutes before the evening meal service after a screaming match with Ilsa right in the dining room."

"It sounds like the two of you need to have a heart-to-heart talk."

Summer shuddered. "I think I'd rather have a root canal without any anesthesia. You know I don't like confrontation, Spring. Besides, it's not my place to tell the director how to operate the place. I've only been volunteering at Manna for a couple of months myself."

"Mmm-hmm," Spring said. "Long enough to see that if things continue the way they're going, there may not *be* a soup kitchen at Common Ground if Ilsa chases or scares off all of the people who are running the place. No one gets paid to be there. Just like no one gets paid at any of the other church ministries. I probably put more hours in at Common Ground's free clinic than I do at the hospital. You know how mom is about the homeless shelter. And you do remember that quote about what happens when a good man—in this case, a good woman—does nothing."

While Summer pondered that, Spring dabbed her fork into the homemade raspberry sauce, then speared a piece of the fruit. "For the record, I didn't make you move home. If you hadn't already been thinking about it, you never would have come," Spring said as Summer gave her an indulgent smile. "Besides, it's good to have you here. It will take the pressure off me with Mom."

Summer rolled her eyes. "Good luck with that. You know that once Lovie Darling gets an idea in her head, there's no stopping her. And the idea that's been stuck there lately is that one of us needs to get married and start providing grandchildren for her to spoil."

The doorbell, a chime that echoed like church bells through the house, halted Spring's response to that taunt.

Summer dabbed her mouth with a napkin and pushed her chair back. "Wonder who that is. I'll be right back."

Without even thinking about it, she pulled a small tube of lip gloss from the pocket of her tailored shorts and refreshed her mouth.

Leaning back in her chair and looking toward the front of the house, Spring observed, "Summer, there's a fire truck outside."

"A fire truck? Oh, dear, I hope nothing's happened to any of the neighbors."

The bell chimed again as Summer reached the front door. She pulled it open without looking through the peep hole to find firemen in full gear on her threshold. A ladder fire truck sat at the curb and a sport utility vehicle with the Cedar Springs, North Carolina Fire Department logo emblazoned on its side was pulled into her driveway.

"Good afternoon," the firefighter in front said. "I'm looking for Summer Spencer."

"I—I'm S-Summer Spencer," she said, her voice quavering almost as much as her heart suddenly pounded. "W-what's happened? Tell me, what's happened?"

"Summer…"

She heard her sister's voice behind her, but Summer only registered the officials standing before her, bringing her more horrifying news. Two of them were dressed in typical firefighter gear and the third, the one who addressed her, was in a dress uniform, the type worn by the brass to deliver condolences to the family of the deceased. In that moment, Summer's hard-won confidence shattered and her sense of security evaporated.

She didn't have the strength to go through it again. Not now. Not when she was finally stable, settled and starting her life over again in a place where the past didn't haunt her days and where people didn't give her pitying glances on the street.

"Summer…"

"No," she said, "no," as darkness enveloped her.

* * *

"Are you sure she's okay?" Cameron Jackson asked.

The beautiful but unconscious woman he'd caught and lifted into his arms was just now stirring on the overstuffed sofa where he'd gently placed her.

His firefighters had sprung into action when she'd collapsed, one dashing to the van for oxygen and the other summoning an ambulance.

"I think so," the efficient blonde said. "She was just a bit overwhelmed."

Just like his firefighters, she didn't panic when the woman fainted; she just reacted—in all the right ways.

"I'm Spring," she told him. "This is my sister. Her name is Summer."

Even given the situation, his mouth quirked up. She saw it.

"Our parents had a, let's just say, unique sense of humor."

Spring was taking her sister's pulse while one of the firefighters got the oxygen flowing and the mask over her nose and mouth.

"Summer? Honey? Can you hear me?"

The pretty blonde tried to sit up and Cameron was quick to assist. He sat beside her offering comfort and aid, and wondering what type of attack she'd had.

In all his years as a firefighter and as chief in Cedar Springs, he'd seen fire victims and their relatives overcome with emotion. But never had he had someone pass out on him simply because he'd said hello.

Now that he could see she was recovering, he took a moment to assess the two women. They were clearly sisters, one a younger version of the other. Both had the porcelain complexions that were evidence of good genes. While dressed casually, the older in chinos, loafers and a white button-down shirt and the other in navy blue shorts and an identical white shirt, they both exuded the aura of wealth.

"W-what happened?"

"Would you get her a glass of water, please?" Spring asked the firefighter. "The kitchen is right around there," she indicated.

"Yes, ma'am, Doctor Darling."

Cameron looked up at her. Doctor? No wonder she hadn't panicked.

As Billy sprinted toward the kitchen, Cameron helped Summer sit up. He stayed close though, afraid that she might faint on him again. A hand at her back held her steady.

"Spring?" she asked.

"Hold on a sec, sis," Spring said as she tucked the ear buds of a stethoscope and took her younger sister's vitals.

"You keep a stethoscope at the ready?" Cameron asked.

Spring smiled. After she finished, she draped the instrument around her neck.

"Some doctors still make house calls," she said.

Cameron looked from one blonde beauty to the other. "You're sisters," he observed.

He could have slapped himself at the obvious remark.

"Give the man a cigar," Spring said. But any bite that could have been in her voice was offset by a smile and a little wink. "Okay, Summer. I think you're going to live."

"*I* might not," Cameron said. "You gave me quite a scare."

The firefighter who had been dispatched to the kitchen handed Summer a glass with ice water. "Here you go, ma'am."

"My mother is 'ma'am.' Please," she said. "Call me Summer."

Summer, Cameron thought. The name suited her. While he momentarily glanced up at the older sister, the doctor, his attention quickly returned to the younger beauty.

As a blush of color rose in her cheeks, a Scripture rose to his mind: *The man who finds a good wife finds a good thing.*

"I don't need this," she said tugging at the oxygen mask. "I'm fine, really."

He watched as she took a sip of water from the glass and handed it back to her sister. She then seemed to notice him and the two firefighters, and her eyes widened in panic.

"What happened?"

"You fainted," Spring said.

Her cheeks got even redder, and this time Cameron suspected that it might be a blush of embarrassment. He wanted, inexplicably, to soothe the tension from her.

"My name is Cameron Jackson," he said. "I'm the fire chief here in Cedar Springs. We," he added with a nod toward the two crewmen with him, "came to check your smoke alarms. You requested the service from the department." He said it almost as a question, something that made the woman smile.

The siren of an ambulance could be heard through the screen of the still open front door.

"Billy, go give them a sitrep."

"Yes, sir." The young firefighter gave a half salute to the two women and dashed toward the door.

"Would you like to go to the hospital?"

"No, there's no need" Summer said, glancing up at Spring. "My sister's a doctor. And I'm sorry. I guess it's not every day that someone falls out over smoke alarm batteries."

Cameron looked up at Spring, the pieces finally falling into place. Spring Darling. She was the doc who worked at the free clinic. They'd never met, but he'd heard of her. What he didn't know was that she had such an enchanting sister.

"You're Dr. Spring Darling," he said.

"Guilty as charged," she said, holding out a hand for him to shake.

He did and was surprised to find that she shook

hands like a man. The grip strong, steady and sure. It was a bit off-putting, but he didn't know why.

"And I'm Summer Spencer," the younger sister said, standing.

The handshakes were as different as the seasons they were named for. Summer's was light, airy and barely there.

Fifteen minutes later, after the paramedics also checked her vitals, the firefighters Billy and Chip and the two emergency medical technicians who had arrived in the ambulance said their farewells, each licking his lips from cheesecake samples and clutching a plastic sandwich bag filled with home-made cookies.

Cameron was about to follow them when he stopped in his tracks. Spring, trailing behind to see him to the door, bumped into him.

"Sorry about that," she said.

He turned.

"What's wrong?"

"We didn't check the smoke alarms."

She grinned.

Summer, her purse slung over one shoulder, shook her head.

"I need to get down to the clinic, sis. First-aid kits and home fire extinguishers are in the kitchen, second shelf, and in the hall linen closet upstairs. My housewarming gifts to her," she added for Cameron's benefit.

"She's the practical one," Summer said dryly.

Ignoring the teasing Spring continued, looking at Summer but talking to Cameron. "I should see Mom at the clinic so I'll call you in about half an hour to confirm the time for Sunday."

Cameron got the subtle but effective warning from the older sister. Spring was leaving him alone with Summer, but would call in thirty minutes. He could appreciate the protectiveness, but also wondered if there might be more to it. She'd fainted at the sight of firefighters on her doorstep. Was that the residual effect of some trauma she'd suffered? Summer had a different last name than her sister. Was she pregnant? Ill? Where was her husband? She wasn't wearing a wedding band, but that didn't mean much to some people these days. Clearly the doctor had concerns, but Cameron kept his questions to himself.

"They took the new resident kits with them," he said. "I'll go grab one from the truck. Your home safety check won't take long."

While the Cedar Springs fire chief roamed through her house, Summer Spencer did what she always did when nervous or upset. She baked. By the time he returned to the kitchen, she had a batch of cookies in the oven and was placing dirty pans and utensils in the dishwasher.

"All done?"

"Yes," he said. "You look good."

When the color rose in her cheeks, he apparently

realized the unintended double entendre. "I mean, the house. Everything is fine with the house. Your batteries are all replaced. Wiring looks… The wiring is fine, too."

Summer took a bit of comfort in the fact that he seemed as uncomfortable as she was.

"So, you're a baker?"

"Oh, no. I just dabble," she said, shutting the dishwasher door and drying her hands on a towel.

"Your cheesecake rivals what's sold over at Sweetings," he said. "My guys and the paramedics left here looking like they'd found the keys to the cookie store."

"Thank you," she said. "Cooking and baking relaxes me."

Years ago, she would have known what to say to this man, a man who so gallantly carried her when she'd fainted as if she were some delicate Southern belle with the vapors. But all that seemed to come from her mouth was inane chatter. She couldn't seem to think straight. As a matter of fact, the only thought in her head was that she didn't want him to go away believing she was a delicate little flower who needed a man's protection. The fact that she'd lived most of her life just like that only spurred her determination to offer him a logical explanation.

The only problem was, well, she didn't exactly have one of those handy.

"I wanted to explain," she said, "about what happened at the door."

He shook his head, cutting off her words. "There's no need," he said. "I'm just glad you got the all-clear from your sister and from the EMTs."

"My sister is a pediatrician. I'm not a child."

"No," he said. "Of course you're not."

Something in his tone arrested her, but before Summer could decipher it or determine just why this man seemed to make her so—was it uncomfortable or just aware?—he'd hefted his bag and was headed to the door. He left a packet of materials on the foyer table next to a bouquet of flowers she'd cut from her garden just that morning. The cover design on the new resident's packet, with a picture of a fire truck said: Welcome Home to Cedar Springs, North Carolina.

As she watched him back the fire department's sport utility vehicle out of her driveway, Summer didn't feel welcomed, and she couldn't help but wonder if she was letting an opportunity slip away.

Chapter Two

At Manna, the Common Ground soup kitchen, Vanessa Gerard peered at the recipe Summer handed her.

"Summer, I can't cook. Honestly, I can't. I burn water when I try to make a cup of tea."

"Vanessa, it's easy. See, just five ingredients and they are all right here. The *mise en place* has already been done. And there are just four steps, easy peasy."

"The meeson what?"

"It means all the ingredients are already prepped. So you don't have to chop or measure anything. Just follow the steps on the recipe."

The brown-skinned woman with the long braids didn't at all look reassured. "We're supposed to be helping these people," Vanessa said, "not giving them food poisoning."

Summer laughed and gave the soup kitchen volunteer a comforting pat on the back. "You're not going to give anyone food poisoning. And you're going to be shocked at how well they turn out."

Vanessa had been coming in a couple of times a week to get out of the house. But this was her first time actually working in the kitchen. She usually served meals to the people who came to Manna at Common Ground. Many of them were homeless and came in for a meal before checking in at the homeless shelter, which was one of four community outreach programs operated by the Common Ground ministry.

The faith-based ministry known as Common Ground was formed by the pastors of three diverse congregations. Its mission was to strengthen Christian ties, unite the churches and to work together in community outreach and service.

Still looking doubtful, Vanessa eyed the recipe. "If you say so."

Confident that the casseroles would be just fine, Summer went to check on the progress of her cookies, and then one of the other volunteers. Just a handful of the volunteers at the soup kitchen came in on regular schedules—a fact she quickly ascertained, so she never knew how many people might be available to help cook on any given day.

That was one of the situations that Ilsa Keller, as director of the soup kitchen, should have addressed. When Summer suggested setting up a schedule, she'd been told that things operated just fine and essentially to mind her own business.

For the Wednesday lunches and dinners, Manna needed at least four helpers in the kitchen, because of the extra baking required for the coffee fellowship after the weekly Bible study. At the volunteers' meeting last month, when Summer noted that Wednesdays were especially strained and could use a dedicated roster of volunteers, Ilsa had shot her down until someone else said the same thing. And then the soup kitchen director had been forced to promise she would consider their suggestions.

But when only two volunteers showed up today, Summer talked Vanessa into assisting in the kitchen.

She grabbed a couple of heavy potholders, and then from one of the two double industrial-sized ovens, pulled out a tray of white chocolate macadamia cookies and an oversized flat pan filled with red velvet bars. She would whip up the creamy vanilla frosting for the bars after they'd cooled and she got the chicken soup on simmer.

"Summer, there's someone here to see you," Mrs. Davidson trilled from the doorway.

Startled, Summer glanced up. "Me? Here?"

The plump woman with the face, voice and disposition of everyone's favorite auntie, smiled. "Yes, dear. Don't keep him waiting."

What *him* would be calling on her, and at the soup kitchen no less?

She placed the baked goods on cooling racks and slipped off the gloved potholders. "I'll be right there," she told Mrs. Davidson. But the woman was already gone.

Pulling the ever-present tube of lip gloss out, she touched up her mouth using the bottom of a baking pan as a mirror, making sure she didn't have flour or some other ingredients on her face, then headed to see who'd come calling.

Summer was stunned to see *him*.

Cameron Jackson, the city fire chief, was at the soup kitchen and had come to see her?

She blushed at the thought that two days ago he'd carried her when she'd actually fainted on him at her front door.

Summer almost didn't recognize him as he stood waiting in the dining hall, near the brick fireplace, wearing jeans and a white T-shirt sporting the Cedar Springs Fire Department logo. He looked like a regular guy, a handsome one, but a regular guy. Gone were the starched and pressed dress blues of his fire chief's uniform. His blond hair looked slightly tousled, as if he'd just run his hands through it.

She looked around to see if someone else might possibly be waiting for her, but they were the only two people in the room. As she approached him, he stepped forward.

"Chief Jackson. This is a surprise."

"Please, call me Cameron."

"Cameron."

She said the name tentatively, as if not quite sure

she wanted to commit to the familiarity of it. She had pretty much spent the last two days trying to get him out of her mind—to no apparent avail.

She'd also tried to put out of her mind the conversation she'd had with her older sister the night of "the incident." Spring had called to check in and see how things had gone. And she'd insisted that Cameron was interested in Summer, interested *that* way, not just as a new city resident.

It had taken a couple of days but Summer had finally stopped thinking about him. And now here he was.

Spring's words came back to her: *He wants to take you out, silly. On a date.*

Summer didn't see it that way. Spring insisted that Summer also hadn't seen the way the fire chief looked at her Monday afternoon when he thought no one was watching, the way he'd gently cradled her and seemed to take a slightly more than professional interest in her.

Summer had countered that his interest was in making sure one of the small city's new residents didn't die on him. Spring just tsk-tsked, and told her to take a chance.

But Summer didn't date. And she surely wouldn't start with someone as…well, as male as Cameron Jackson.

He was muscular, not bulked up like a body-builder, but he possessed a strength and a sturdiness that said he was used to being a protector. She'd already noticed his dark blond hair, and now she took in his eyes, an easy blue that was comforting in an odd way—odd, because she didn't need any comforting, at least not now.

"May I call you Summer?"

She noticed his eyes also seemed to light up when he talked.

"Y-yes. Everyone calls me Summer. My sisters are Spring, Autumn and Winter. Our parents had something of a twisted sense of humor. We were teased about it when we were younger. But now…"

Realizing that she was babbling, she closed her mouth, clasped her hands together and stared at the floor.

"I brought something for you," he said, walking toward one of the long dining tables. The tables were already dressed for the evening meal with linens and functional centerpieces—clear bowls filled with apples, oranges and bananas for their guests to help themselves.

Her heart tripped a bit. He brought her a present?

"Well, for you to use," he said, clarifying as if she'd spoken the question aloud.

Oh, dear. Had she?

"We've been collecting food over at the station houses," he said. "I've tried to set a standard without preaching at the crews. Every time one of the guys uses profanity, he has to pay up with a canned good or non-perishable item that gets donated to Manna. I figured that would be an easy way to get the message across about the language while doing something helpful for the community."

Summer glanced down at the half-filled brown paper bag.

"Congratulations. Looks like it's working since you only have a few items."

Cameron groaned.

"This is just what I carried in," he said. "There are three big boxes in the truck."

"Oh."

"Yeah," he said. "Oh."

An awkward silence fell between them. Summer didn't know what to do with her hands. She'd been so long removed from the dating scene that she had no clue about how to act. Plus, Cameron made her nervous, like a filly not yet acquainted with the new trainer at a stable.

But the manners she and her sisters learned at Lovie Darling's School of Raising the Seasons kicked in when Summer's feminine wiles deserted her.

"Would you like…"

"I guess I should get…"

They both started at the same time.

"I'm sorry," she said. "You go first."

He put his hands in his jeans pockets and rocked back on his feet. "I was just going to say, I'll go get the other donations."

"I was going to ask if you'd like a cup of coffee. I just took cookies out of the oven."

His face lit up.

"If you think I'm going to pass up that offer, you need to think again," he said. "I'll be right back."

As Cameron hauled the boxed items to the kitchen, Summer put on a fresh pot of coffee and plated up a few of the white chocolate macadamia nut cookies.

He wants to take you out, silly. On a date.

Her older sister's words echoed in Summer's mind. Was that why he'd come himself instead of sending someone to deliver the donations?

By the time he got everything stowed in the receiving area of the big kitchen, she was waiting with steaming mugs of coffee, a plate of cookies... and a crowd. There with Summer was Mrs. Davidson from the Common Ground office, and a petite woman he didn't immediately recognize.

Trying to get a few moments alone with Summer Spencer was more difficult than herding cats. If he hadn't seen a spark of interest in her eyes, he would think she was trying to shield herself from his attention.

After she'd fainted in his arms and he'd taken some good-natured teasing at the station house about beautiful blondes falling down at the mere sight of him, he'd discreetly asked around and found out that she had just recently moved home to North Carolina from somewhere farther south, in Georgia. Instead of settling in at what was known as the Darling Compound, she'd purchased her own home.

The part he hadn't bargained on was that Summer Spencer, the delicate blonde with the sad eyes and the killer baking skills, was a Darling, of the Darlings of Cedar Springs. The very wealthy, very cultured, pillars of town society Darlings.

"Chief Jackson, this is Doris Davidson and Samantha Burns, one of our volunteers."

"Oh, the chief and I know each other," Mrs. Davidson said. "How are you today?" she asked before taking a sampling of a cookie.

"Just fine, Mrs. D."

The woman named Samantha wore an apron that had the Common Ground logo on the front. "Hello, there. Are you the chief of police or something?"

"Fire chief," Cameron said.

"Oh, my goodness, Summer. These are excellent," exclaimed Mrs. Davidson. "Would you be willing to make a couple dozen for me for my book group? I host next week and I was just going to get something from Sweetings. These are so much better."

"You know I will, Mrs. Davidson," Summer said. "Just tell me when you need them."

She offered a small paper plate with two cookies to Cameron. "How do you take your coffee?"

"Black," he said.

Vanessa Gerard joined them a moment later. "I

got the pans in the oven," she said. "It was easy. I may try that at home."

"Told you," Summer said. "We're taking a little break," she said, serving up another plate with cookies to Vanessa. "Would you like coffee?"

"No, thanks," Vanessa said. "Trying to cut back. Howzit going, Chief Cam?"

"Well, Vanessa. What about with you?"

She lifted a brow, gave a slight shrug and said, "It's going."

"You'll let me know?" he asked.

Vanessa gave an exasperated sigh. "I always do, chief."

"I'm holding you to that," Cameron said.

Summer noted the easy familiarity between them and the nickname Vanessa used. A stab of jealousy or possibly disappointment shot through her. She had no claim on Cameron Jackson so she wasn't at all sure from whence it sprang.

Mrs. Davidson, not recognizing the bit of tension that seemed to suddenly envelop the room, piped up. "I declare, Summer, the best thing that ever happened to Manna at Common Ground was you showing up when you did."

Not willing to acknowledge her private reaction to Cameron and Vanessa, Summer gave Mrs. Davidson a sunny smile.

"Yes," Vanessa said. "Mrs. D is right. Because if you hadn't walked in here, they were going to dragoon me and that would have truly been a disaster in the making."

Cameron glanced at his watch, then put down his coffee cup. "Summer, may I have a word with you?"

She glanced at the other three women as if looking for validation. "Uh, sure."

Vanessa took in the boxes neatly stacked on the receiving bench. "Did you bring those, Chief Cam?"

When he nodded, Vanessa snagged another cookie from the cooling rack then reached for a clipboard dangling under the counter on an unseen hook. "That's something I *can* do—log in donations."

"Come along, dear," Mrs. Davidson told Samantha Burns. "Break's over. We have quite a bit to do before our guests arrive."

With thanks to Summer for the cookies and their goodbyes to the fire chief, the two hustled off. Vanessa went to tend to the donations from the fire department and Cameron steered Summer back toward the dining hall for a few words in private.

His arm brushed hers as he held the door open and Summer's breath caught at the unexpected contact. If he noticed, he didn't let on. He was probably just happy she didn't pass out on him again.

She told herself to stop acting like a ninny. She was twenty-eight years old, not sixteen.

In the dining hall, he pulled out a chair at one of the tables and held it out for her to be seated.

Appreciating the small gesture, Summer murmured a "thank you" as he settled in the seat next to her.

"I wanted to see how you were doing," he said.

Oh, great, she thought. *He thinks I'm an invalid.* Inexplicably, she wanted to explain.

"Thank you again," she said, "for what you did the other day. It was a reflex, I think. I thought something was wrong. You all caught me by surprise."

Cameron smiled. "Have dinner with me tonight."

"I beg your pardon?"

The abrupt change of topic more than startled her. "Dinner? Us. Together."

She shook her head slightly. "I don't think that's a good idea."

"Why?"

She wanted to explain. Dinner meant they would be out together. On a date. But Summer couldn't date. Didn't date. And the explanation she'd been all ready to give him fled from her brain, right along with her courage.

"I'm…" she swallowed and got a hold of her tongue if not her suddenly racing heart. "My husband might not approve."

Chapter Three

The stricken look on his face convicted her.

"You're married?"

His gaze dipped to her left hand resting on the table. Self-conscious, she put both ringless hands in her lap.

Taking a deep breath, Summer decided that being open and honest about her situation was her best course of action.

"Chief Jackson, I want to explain something to you."

He leaned back in his chair and folded his arms. But a moment later, he sighed and released the defensive gesture.

Offering a tremulous smile, Summer got her thoughts together. It wasn't so much that she wanted to open up on this, she *needed* to. Enough time had passed, and moving home to Cedar Springs was her big step toward reclaiming her life.

"Seeing you and your men on my doorstep," she

began, "was a shock. A bad shock to my system. I'd truly forgotten about the new resident's home safety check I'd requested."

She swallowed, took a ragged breath and then offered up a little prayer for strength.

"The last time men in uniform came to my front door, it was to tell me that my husband had been killed."

His eyes widened and he reached for her hands in a comforting gesture. But before he could offer the obligatory, "I'm sorry" condolences, she rushed on.

"It's coming on two years," she said. "I moved home to start a new chapter in my life. I sold our place in Macon and bought the house here, a house where I could make new memories instead of dwelling on the past. Seeing you, the three of you," she quickly clarified, "standing there looking official, well, it just derailed me a bit."

She took a deep breath, hoping that he understood, even while she acknowledged to herself that dumping baggage at his feet was not a good way to win friends and influence people.

There was something comforting about this man. Unlike some people who listened long enough to gauge when and where they could break in with their own words and experiences, he seemed to listen to her with his whole body.

That, Summer decided, was both comforting and disconcerting.

* * *

Cameron felt like a heel.

So much made sense now. The protectiveness of her sister at the house. The uncertainty he sensed in Summer. The almost-sadness of her eyes. He had known that she'd moved to North Carolina from Georgia, but had come to the erroneous conclusion that the move home was to be near family, not to escape her grief.

"I'm sorry," he said. "I'm very sorry for your loss, and for rushing you."

Summer shook head. "That's just it, you weren't rushing me. I should be," she gave a little shrug, "I guess you'd say, 'over it' by now."

This time he did clasp her hands in his. "You never get over losing someone special," he said.

She smiled this time. Then extricated her hands from his.

"Thank you for asking me out," she said. "But the answer is still…"

"Shh," he said, cutting her off before she could finish. "I know."

Summer pushed back her chair and rose, the movement graceful.

"I really need to get back to work," she told him. "We're shorthanded today. Vanessa and Samantha are the only two volunteers who showed up, and I borrowed Samantha from Mrs. D, who really needs her in the office."

He rose, as well, and escorted Summer back to

the kitchen, where a buzzer was going off and Vanessa was struggling to get a handle on a big pot that seemed to be boiling over.

"Oh, dear. That's the stock for the chicken soup."

Cameron rushed forward and gave Vanessa a hand by moving the pot to another burner on the industrial-sized stove. Summer turned off the timer that was set on a continuous buzz, then slipped on a pair of thick pot-holder gloves and went to one of the ovens. As she pulled out a pan, Cameron came forward.

"Is that a turkey?" he asked, amazement in his voice.

He spied some dish towels on the prep counter and used them to safeguard his hands as he took over the lifting for her. "Here, I'll get that."

"Thanks," Summer said, relinquishing the task to him. "And yes, it's a turkey. There are two more in the bottom ovens. Both are ready to come out, too, if you don't mind."

Cameron knew about the soup kitchen: it was one of four ongoing ministries operated by Common Ground, the coalition formed by three congregations in Cedar Springs. As a member of The Fellowship, he regularly contributed to Common Ground. And as fire chief, he knew the buildings where the homeless shelter, the free clinic and the soup kitchen were located, but he'd never actually been to any of them, just the recreation center where he sometimes played baseball with a youth league.

"How many people do you cook for?" Cameron asked.

"We never really know, but on average about ninety to a hundred, sometimes more, especially on Wednesdays, when there's also the Bible study and snacks afterward."

"And you're cooking for a hundred people, just the two of you?"

Summer shrugged. "We do what has to be done. And reinforcements will be in closer to serving time. I came in early to get the turkeys going. They're actually for sandwiches on Thursday."

Cameron found himself walloped somewhere between amazed and dismayed. He'd come here on his morning off to see Summer Spencer, taking over the food donation delivery duty because it gave him a legitimate excuse to show up at Manna.

Now he realized that maybe it wasn't just for his own selfish reasons that he was here at this time and place. He was *supposed* to be here today.

The Lord worked in mysterious ways.

He got the first large turkey out of the oven and onto a counter where Summer indicated, then he pulled out the others.

As Summer went to work pouring ingredients into a large mixer, Cameron watched her. Every movement was efficient. She worked with a grace that almost seemed like a ballet, reaching for this, adding that. No movement was wasted.

Vanessa was chopping carrots.

Across the room, he spied Common Ground aprons similar to the one Vanessa wore. He claimed one of them and tied it on, then pulled out his cell phone and made a call.

When he finished he pocketed the phone, went to a sink where he washed and dried his hands. Then he came up beside Summer.

"How can I help?"

"Miss Summer, you make me happy to be homeless," an elderly black man known only as Sweet Willie said.

"Brother Willie, what a thing to say," she replied, tucking an extra cookie for him into a small paper bag.

"This the best food I've ever eaten. Thank you kindly."

Summer beamed. "I'm glad you enjoyed the meal, Brother Willie."

He shuffled out the door, the last of their guests to depart.

For the first time since that morning, she exhaled. Summer had had her doubts about how they were going to pull off the meal. In Summer's two months with Manna, she'd yet to see the soup kitchen's director on their busiest day. Ilsa Keller was great at promoting Manna in the community, but that ambassadorship apparently came at the expense of actually managing the day-to-day operation of the place.

If it hadn't been for Cameron Jackson and the two guys he'd talked into coming over to help, she wasn't sure if they would have had everything ready by the time people started arriving at four o'clock.

Six Common Ground volunteers had arrived at about three-thirty to act as servers, but they wouldn't have had anything to serve if Cameron hadn't pitched in. She still didn't know who the two guys were—personal friends of his or firefighters he'd ordered to come help. He'd simply introduced them and told them to do whatever Summer said. She'd been too grateful and too busy to inquire.

"That was a nice thing for him to say."

Summer smiled.

For some reason, she wasn't at all surprised to find Cameron at her side. They'd worked as a team today, serving and ministering. It gave her a new insight into the fire chief. Most men would have bolted after a woman's rejection of a dinner date.

She studied him for a moment. Cameron wasn't just trying to get to know her. She'd seen him talking and then praying with a couple people after the meal began. Many of them knew him and called him Chief Cam, just as Vanessa had done.

Just who was Cameron Jackson?

"He hasn't been here for a couple of weeks," she said, telling him about Sweet Willie. "I was starting to worry that something had happened to him. I asked around, but none of our regulars knew where he was."

"You do good work," Cameron said. "I'm going to let Pastor Hines—Rick Hines is the lead pastor at my church, The Fellowship," he said, clarifying for her. "I'm going to let him know that Manna needs some dedicated volunteers in the early part of the day. I'm sure there are folks in the congregation who can help."

Summer bit her tongue. She would not bad-mouth the program at Manna. Yes, things could be done differently, but it wasn't her place to harp on all the shortcomings.

"Today was an anomaly," she said. "I'm glad you and your friends came to the rescue. Thank you."

They made their way to the kitchen where the cleanup crew was turning the space back into a sparkling setup for the next day's volunteers and setting out items for the early morning prep.

At some point between serving chicken soup and rolls, Summer had decided that a date with a man who would give the homeless almost seven hours of his day was a date she'd like to go on.

Summer retrieved her handbag, said good-night to those who remained and let Cameron escort her out the back door and toward her car in the parking lot behind Manna at Common Ground.

"If the offer is still open," she said, "I would like to have dinner with you."

Chapter Four

"Really?"

The grin transformed his face into one of boyish delight.

She smiled back. "Yes, really."

"How about Friday night?" Cameron asked.

Summer willed herself to ignore the apprehension that raced through her and to savor the unfamiliar thrill of anticipation. She would have two days to get herself together emotionally. But right now, this felt right.

"Friday night sounds terrific," she heard herself say, and could only wonder about the breathless tone that seemed to accompany the words.

"I can pick you up at your house," Cameron said. "I think I know where you live."

He kept a straight face for half a beat and then chuckled as a blush blossomed on Summer.

"I can explain…"

He halted her words with a finger at his lips. "Summer, I told you. You don't owe me any explanations."

Suddenly feeling a bit like the Summer she used to be years ago, she cocked her head a bit and gave him a saucy smile.

"So," she said, "aren't you at all curious about why I changed my mind?"

He winked at her. "Woman's prerogative," he said. "That is definitely something I have learned to respect."

That earned him a laugh. He held his hand out to her and she took it. The gesture, old-fashioned and sweet, made her smile.

"Thank you," she said as they headed toward the vehicle she indicated. "For everything you did today. I really, really appreciated the help."

He nodded. "I hope to get you some permanent help. I'm going to let Pastor Hines know that more than financial contributions are needed here. You and Mrs. D should not have to scramble the way you did today."

Summer was pretty sure that what she was hearing was unique. Not every man would see a problem and immediately seek a solution. Maybe that was why he was the fire chief at such a young age. She pegged him as being in his mid-thirties, and that was being generous. She was pretty sure that police and fire chiefs were supposed to be much older, men and women with gray hair at the temples and grandchildren they liked to spoil when they were off duty.

"Thank you," she simply said.

"May I call you?"

She smiled, liking the chivalrousness that he seemed to exude, sort of like an old Southern gentleman. "Yes, you may."

She gave him her cell number.

"It has a Georgia area code," she said. "I haven't transferred it to a North Carolina one, and my friends there..." she faltered, then shook her head. "I'm sure you don't want to hear about all that."

"I'll call you tomorrow."

They stood there, the moment awkward as neither seemed to know quite how to conclude the conversation.

In the end, it was Cameron who found the way. He leaned forward, kissed her on the cheek and said, "I'm looking forward to Friday."

Hours later, Summer still felt that kiss and wondered just what she had agreed to.

A date!

She sat in her bedroom at the vanity second-guessing herself, fretting and in a state her mother would describe as working herself into a tizzy.

The good thing about being back home in Cedar Springs was that when she wanted or needed to connect with one of her sisters, it could be face-to-face, instead of long distance from Georgia to North Carolina.

She glanced around, looking for the phone. The house on Hummingbird Lane was in pristine condition. It was nothing at all like the Greek Revival McMansion that she and Garrett had called home back in Macon. No professional decorator had come through with a horde of minions designing the house for maximum impact or with an eye toward the critical review of country club wives. She sold the Macon house fully furnished, taking with her just a few sentimental pieces and the antique furniture that had been passed down to her from her grandmother.

This house, her new home, was spacious but not ostentatious. And the only interior decorators who had crossed its threshold were her sisters. That was why she had no idea where the phone was. One of them put it somewhere that Summer did not consider intuitive.

Summer sighed.

She knew it was not the missing telephone that bothered her. That was just symbolic of her life at the moment: not where she thought it would be.

What really bothered her was what she had agreed to do with Cameron Jackson.

A date.

She was going on a date!

Summer didn't know what was scarier: the idea of a social engagement with a man she had, for all intents and purposes, just met, or the very notion of going out. It almost felt as if she were cheating on Garrett. Intellectually, she knew that made no sense. It had been almost two years since her world imploded around her. Almost two years since she'd buried the one man she thought she would spend the rest of her life with, the man she had exchanged holy vows of matrimony with. *For better or worse, in sickness and health, until death do we part.*

How was she to know—how could she have ever even imagined— that those vows did not guarantee them fifty years of wedded bliss?

Instead of heading out on their highly anticipated tour and cruise of Italy to celebrate their fourth wedding anniversary, at twenty-six years old, Summer was burying her husband. She felt the sharp sting of approaching tears.

Stop it, Summer. Just stop.

Refusing to give in to the temptation to wallow in self-pity, she snatched up a tube of mascara and refreshed her eyes even though she wasn't going anywhere.

Feeling a little better, she got up and plucked her cell phone from her purse. Spring would still be with patients at the free clinic, but maybe Autumn had a few minutes to spare for a sister who was acting like a total spaz.

As the phone rang, she walked around her bedroom trying to figure out where the receiver for the landline telephone might be. The Darling sisters and their mother had taken over the house, throwing themselves into making Summer's new home as comfortable and cozy as possible.

They had done a good job.

As Summer headed into her large walk-in closet, Autumn's mobile phone went straight to voice mail.

Summer sighed.

Instead of continuing the search for the landline, she decided to stare at her clothes and try to figure out what was appropriate to wear out on a date with Fire Chief Cameron Jackson.

He had not said where they would be going, but she had a general idea. Dinner and a movie were typical first-date fare. And unless he planned something for them to do in Raleigh, the options in Cedar Springs were pretty much limited to movies or bowling and eating.

For a town its size, Cedar Springs, North Carolina, boasted an eclectic mix of restaurants. Everything from traditional Southern fare and Americana to national chains and the nouveau cuisine that might be associated with large cities like New York or Washington, D.C., could be found either in town or nearby.

Cameron looked like a Carolina barbeque kind of guy.

That thought made her smile.

Something about his rugged good looks made her think he wouldn't object to a pig-picking backyard barbeque. She could imagine him enjoying the food, not minding if barbeque sauce dripped on his shirt.

The contrast with Dr. Garrett Spencer or even Dr. John Darling, her father, could not have been greater. If it were true that little girls grew up and married men just like their fathers, the case had certainly proven true with Summer.

When Autumn said as much, Summer denied it. Now, however, with Garrett gone, she did see the similarities between the man who raised her and the man she married. Both were physicians dedicated to their professions and their patients. Both doted on their wives, providing the wealth that made outside employment for their spouses the stuff of hobbies and volunteer work.

Summer knew it was true that her oldest sister, Spring, had taken after their father by going into medicine, while Summer tended to hearth and home, much like their mother, Lovie Darling. Lovie's example had been one of quiet grace, Southern gentility and charm, and a strong faith enhanced with a healthy sense of humor.

From her mother, Summer inherited the domestic gene. Autumn and Winter called themselves the changelings, because beyond physical attributes, neither of them seemed to carry the traits of either parent.

Summer was pretty sure that Cameron Jackson was interested in her because he had not yet met Autumn. Her little sister was the Darling daughter who wowed everyone she met: men, women, teen-agers and even little kids. Autumn knew how to bring people together. Spring was the healer and organizer of the bunch, championing causes and making things happen. Winter was always on a quest, off exploring or doing something slightly dangerous. But Summer, well, she was basically a boring homebody, content in the kitchen, tending to her garden flowers and being known as a gracious hostess.

She sighed.

Compared to her sisters' lives, hers was vapid.

And without the social connections she had taken for granted in Macon and Atlanta—being a doctor's wife—she was home in Cedar Springs but felt much like a fish out of water. She had her sisters, of course, but had yet to make many new friends.

Lovie had already tried to set her up with a radiologist who was the son of one of her church members.

That hadn't gone well, but Summer suspected he would be just the first of many eligible men her mother sent her way. Lovie Darling gathered business cards of single professional men the way some women collected recipes. She then parceled the business cards out to her daughters, none too subtly suggesting that she wanted her four daughters married and producing grandchildren for her to spoil.

And now, less than two weeks since the radiologist debacle, she was going out on a date with a man she had just met—a man who was not a whit like her father or her husband.

What was she thinking?

Her cell phone rang as if to answer the question.

"Hello, this is Summer Spencer."

"You know, you don't have to announce who you are. What if it's someone on the other end that you don't ever want to talk to?"

Summer smiled. She left her closet and moved back into the bedroom where she settled on a chaise near the large bay window.

"That, little sister, is because, unlike you, I do not live a life that requires me to be in hiding from some people."

"Hey, I resent that," Autumn declared. "I do not hide. I just don't feel like being bothered with some folks sometimes."

"Is that why you let my call go to voice mail?"

"You wound me, Summer. I did no such thing. I was actually in the shower. Just finished racquetball and tried out a Zumba class a friend was teaching."

Summer shook her head. "You make me tired just listening to you."

"There's a half marathon coming up in six weeks. It's gonna be down in Fayetteville. Lots of cute soldiers from Fort Bragg will be running in it. I can fast-track train you and get you ready to join me."

"I think all of that physical activity has cut off

the oxygen to your brain. Sweat and I do not go together."

Autumn laughed.

Summer heard the chirp of Autumn's car door as the electronic lock disengaged.

"Where are you headed?"

"I was gonna grab a bite to eat, then crash."

"I have quiche."

"You have any of that raspberry cheesecake that you made for Spring left?"

"I didn't make it specifically for her, I just made it."

"Whatever. She got first cut and that's just wrong."

"A big slice will be waiting for you."

Autumn let out a triumphant whoop. "Hah! Guilt trip works every time."

Summer laughed at her sister's antics. "See you in a bit. And, Autumn?"

"Yeah?"

"Drive carefully, please. No texting while driving."

"Bye, worrywart. Oh, hey! Summer!"

Summer held the phone away from her ear. "What?"

"I want to hear about this fire chief that you've been making googly eyes at."

Googly eyes?

Summer was pretty sure she had not made googly eyes with anyone since Jason Weathersby in third grade.

"Well, uh, that is sort of why I called you, Autumn," she confessed. "I have a date with that fire chief."

The cheer that came over the phone line really may have damaged Summer's ears.

Chapter Five

Cameron could not believe she had changed her mind, but he was sure glad of it. While he'd teased Summer Spencer about not needing to know the reason why, he *was* a bit curious. He had enjoyed watching her interact with the homeless and indigent who flocked to Manna at Common Ground. On at least a couple of occasions throughout the evening, he'd caught her looking at him.

He wondered what she saw. Although he had his father's blond hair and blue eyes, he knew he was not considered classically handsome. Cameron was a battle-scarred army veteran who had caught more than his share of bad burns while fighting fires, first during his enlistment and then as a civilian.

The buddies he'd summoned to help out at Manna, on the other hand, had the good looks that seemed to attract women.

In between cooking and serving, he had managed to keep an eye on the pretty blonde who had captivated him from the moment she collapsed in his arms. And the one thing he noticed as Manna at Common Ground's guests arrived—and as his friends ogled her!—was that Summer seemed completely oblivious to his friends' efforts to catch her eye.

A stab of jealousy arced through Cam until he realized that Summer gave his buddy Rob the same gracious and polite treatment that she gave everyone.

Was he just imagining a warmth that seemed to come into her eyes when he himself spoke with her?

He didn't know, but he was grateful and happy that she had agreed to go out with him.

"Chief?"

Cameron started, then focused in on the room. He was in a special meeting of the Cedar Springs City Council and the department heads. While not a regularly scheduled meeting, this one was open to the public because they were discussing town business. A handful of residents sat in the audience.

A few people exchanged amused glances.

"I'm sorry," Cameron said. "What was your question?"

"We wanted to make sure you can meet with the architect when he comes in," Mayor Bernadette Howell said. "We haven't even seen the plans for the development project, let alone voted on anything, and there's already been an uproar in some parts of the city. I keep getting an earful about destroying historic sites and overburdening emergency services, especially the fire department."

Cameron nodded, making a note on his smartphone. "What's that date?"

"Gloria will set you up with an appointment," the mayor said.

Cameron nodded toward the town clerk who doubled as administrative assistant to both the mayor and deputy mayor.

Mayor Howell then asked the city manager for an update on the title search for the two properties under consideration for a new mixed-use residential and retail development.

"The surveyors will be starting some preliminary work in the next few weeks. There's some ambiguity with a few of the parcels that are either adjacent to or possibly that overlap with the Darling land."

The mayor sighed.

As the late meeting went on around him, Cameron's thoughts had been on Summer Spencer more than the new development proposed for Cedar Springs.

Darling land? Wasn't Summer Spencer's sister's last name Darling?

"John, what do you mean overlap?" Cameron asked.

"That's my question, as well," the mayor said.

"Apparently, there were some, er, shall we say gentlemen's agreements regarding property lines many, many decades ago," the city manager said.

"Great," Mayor Howell muttered. "Just great."

"I foresee trouble," a voice rumbled from the end of the table.

"Well, let's not buy trouble before we have to," the mayor snapped. "Everything is preliminary right now. All we're doing is assessing potential sites," she said.

"I, for one, would rather not get into a protracted land dispute with Lovie Darling."

Everyone turned toward Joe Marchand, who had been on the City Council longer than its youngest members had been alive. Joe kept getting re-elected despite his protestations that there were others who should take over the seat. Since he rarely had anything to say at the council meetings, when he did speak, people tended to pay attention.

Cameron leaned toward the police chief, who always sat next to him in council meetings. "Who is Lovie Darling?"

"Old money," the police chief whispered back. "Her husband's family basically founded the town that became Cedar Springs."

Cameron sat back frowning.

He'd been excited about the prospect of taking out Summer Spencer. Now that he suspected she was one of the wealthy Darlings, he wondered how he could beg off from the date.

The last thing he wanted was the high-maintenance drama that went along with a wealthy woman. He'd been down that road once before and it had led straight to misery—and divorce. He didn't plan to head down that path ever again.

When Summer opened her front door, Autumn was not alone. She had somehow managed to round up both Spring and Winter.

Summer groaned. "I knew I should have kept my mouth shut."

"Too late," Autumn said, barging in with a take-out drinks tray.

"Starbucks?"

"What else? She mainlines the stuff," Winter said, following with a small cloth satchel.

Summer nodded toward it. "And what is your contribution to this little intervention?"

"It is *not* an intervention," Spring said. "It's a little sisterly chat. We haven't had one of those in a while."

"And since I am apparently the only person on the planet who doesn't know about this man you're seeing," Winter said, "I expect to be fully filled in and compensated for the misdemeanor of leaving me out of the loop."

Summer groaned as she shut the front door behind her sisters, who all headed to the room their mother had dubbed The Salon.

Overstuffed chintz chairs, lamps with frilly-edged shades and plenty of pillows in coordinating solids and clashing floral prints made it a room ideally suited for chitchats and tea among girlfriends or for snuggling in with a cozy mystery novel on a rainy day.

Summer noted, not for the first time, that her style and those of her sisters varied widely. If they didn't actually resemble each other, no one would imagine they were related.

Spring, in crisp khaki slacks, penny loafers and a white button-down shirt, had clearly come straight from the free clinic. All that was missing was her white doctor's jacket and a stethoscope.

Autumn sported black yoga pants, a T-shirt in bright fuchsia and black flats. And, as always, Autumn's thick blond hair was pulled into a ponytail, with a baseball cap to top it off.

Winter was the surprise today. She had on a tiny floral print sundress that hugged her curves and suspiciously looked like it had come straight from Summer's closet.

"I am not *seeing* him," Summer declared. "I just agreed to go on a date with him Friday night. And, excuse me, but is that my dress?"

"Uh-huh," Autumn said.

At the same time, Winter added, "It's way too big for you."

"She borrowed it when we were doing your bedroom," Autumn the tattletale added. "Where's my raspberry cheesecake?"

"There's cheesecake?" Winter said. "Nobody ever tells me anything."

"Chief Jackson enjoyed it," Spring said, a slight smile at her mouth. Autumn and Winter whirled around.

Summer gasped and threw a tasseled pillow at Spring. "You're supposed to be on my side in this!"

Spring winked at her. "Sorry, couldn't resist."

Summer pouted but couldn't maintain it. She stared at her sisters and her eyes filled with tears.

"I'm so glad I came home. I've missed you guys more than you know."

A moment later, the four Darling sisters shared a group hug full of tears and laughter.

"Just because we're all cozy here," Autumn said breaking free of the circle, "don't for a minute think you're getting any of my cheesecake, Winter."

After they were all settled with either quiche or dessert, coffees and tea, Winter got down to business. "Since everybody except me knows about this guy of hers, who is going to fill me in?"

"He's not *my* guy," Summer said, feeling a need to defend herself.

The others turned to Spring. Autumn and Winter knew that as the oldest and most level-headed of the four, she would tell the truth.

"I was here when they met," Spring said. "Chief Jackson came over to inspect the smoke alarms."

"Is he cute?" Autumn asked.

Summer blushed.

"Oh, he is! Look at her! What does he look like, Spring?"

"I would guess he's about your age, Winter. Mid-thirties. Dark blond hair. Blue eyes. He has that boy-next-door look about him, but a boy next door who had responsibility thrust on him at an early age."

Three sets of arched eyebrows turned in Spring's direction.

"What an astute observation," Summer murmured before taking a sip of tea.

"Did you change specialties to psychology?" Autumn asked.

"No," Summer said aloud. "She's right. That's it. He has an air of responsibility, like he's used to taking care of people."

"Cameron?" Autumn said coughing, as the coffee she was drinking went down the wrong way.

"Should I call an ambulance?" Spring asked dryly.

"Ha, ha," Autumn said. "Cameron? Cameron Jackson?"

"You know him?" Winter and Summer asked at the same time.

"Of course," Autumn said.

Summer's tummy did a little tumble. If Autumn knew Cameron, her chances with him were suddenly diminished.

"I just didn't put that whole chief thing in place until now. You're dating Chief Cam? Way to go, Summer. He's a really good guy. God, country and firefighting."

She went back to forking up cheesecake.

Winter huffed. "Well, don't just leave it hanging there. Spill!"

"Spill what?" Autumn said around bites. She shrugged. "Like I said, he's a stand-up kind of guy. He plays basketball with the kids at the rec center every couple of weeks. The kids really like him."

"Is he cute?" Winter said.

Autumn said, "Yeah, he looks like he means business."

Summer frowned. "What kind of description is that?"

"Focus, please," Winter demanded. "He came here to check Summer's smoke alarm batteries and then what?"

Summer and Spring shared a glance.

And in that moment, Summer knew that her older sister would keep her secret. The fewer people who knew about her fainting, the better—and the less likely it would get back to their mother, who would fuss and probably set up temporary residence in the guest room.

"She was baking and gave the crew cheesecake and cookies," Spring reported.

"You go, sis," Autumn said. "The way to a man's heart is through his stomach. With your baking and cooking, you'll have him literally eating out of your hands in no time."

Summer had a question burning in her. If she failed to ask it now, she knew she might regret it.

"So, you and he aren't…you know…?"

Autumn's eyes widened. "Me and Chief Cam? Goodness, no. He's like the big brother I didn't have. Chief Cam, he's like everybody's big brother. The kids love it when he plays ball with them. And, like I said, he's the all-American kind of guy."

"Apparently, he's not everybody's big brother," Winter observed with a grin. "He clearly doesn't see our Summer as a little sister."

The blush that she thought had dissipated bloomed again on Summer's cheeks.

"So, where are you guys going?"

"I don't know," Summer said. "And I don't know what to wear."

"No twinsets!" Autumn and Winter yelled at the same time.

Summer glared at them.

"And nothing starched," Spring added. "Like those shorts you're wearing."

"What's wrong with neat and pressed clothing?" Summer asked.

"It's a date, not a committee meeting at the library," Autumn said.

"I would not wear shorts to any meeting," Summer declared. "And you three are not helping. What to wear is the least of my problems."

Winter reached over and snatched the last forkful of Autumn's raspberry cheesecake.

"Hey! Foul. Flag on the play!"

Laughing at her sisters, Summer rose and headed to the kitchen.

"The good thing about stress is that I make good use of it," she said.

She returned with a tray bearing four dessert plates, forks and a double chocolate cheesecake.

"How is it you can bake all these sweets and not ever gain an ounce?" Winter asked.

As the curviest of the Darling sisters, every bite she put in her mouth landed on her hips. And unlike Autumn, who lived for every sport ever invented, Winter didn't work off the calories with physical activity.

"That's because I make sure that other people eat it all. So eat up, ladies."

Summer and her sisters spent the next hour talking, laughing and teasing each other.

When she finally closed the door and turned off the downstairs lights to head to bed, Summer realized that not one of her sisters had expressed concern about her dating.

She smiled.

Maybe it was because of the man she had decided to see: a blond-haired, blue-eyed, stand-up kind of guy by the name of Cameron Jackson. Both Spring and Autumn had given him the A-OK. Now all Summer had to do was make it through the date without embarrassing herself.

Chapter Six

It had taken Cameron less than ten minutes on Google and the Cedar Springs Gazette's website to find that Summer Darling Spencer and her sisters were indeed the trust-fund debutantes of Cedar Springs society. The ordeal that had been his two-year marriage to a trust-fund daddy's girl had left him with no illusions about what it meant to be in an economically lopsided relationship. The melding of working class and upper class was the stuff of oil and water, and Cameron had the emotional scars to prove it.

Summer was pretty and he'd been drawn to her vulnerability. But self-preservation trumped those assets.

Cameron's first instinct was to text Summer and tell her something had come up and he wouldn't be able to make it Friday night. But a text message was the coward's way out. He'd all but chased her to get her to agree to go out with him, practically cornering her while she did her volunteer work at Manna at Common Ground.

His mother had raised him to be a gentleman. And a gentleman didn't run away from tough situations. So approaching the business entrance to Manna at Common Ground the next day, the irony didn't escape him that the way his social life was at the moment, he considered breaking a date with a beautiful woman as a tough situation.

Cameron didn't know if she was at the soup kitchen on Thursday, but it was an easy visit for him to make from the public safety building.

As he pulled open the door to the Common Ground business office, he had one goal: extricate himself from the date with Summer Spencer.

"Chief Cam," Mrs. Davidson trilled from her desk. "What a surprise. Two days in a row. To what do we owe the pleasure?"

Doris Davidson was one of a handful of full-time employees for the Common Ground ministries. She was the central receptionist, point person and general bookkeeper for the soup kitchen, recreation center, homeless shelter and free clinic.

"Hi, Mrs. D. Is Summer Spencer working today?"

She gave him a sly smile. "As a matter of fact, she is. I think you know where to find her," Mrs. D said with a general wave in the rear direction.

"Thank you," he said, making his way toward the kitchen.

As he drew closer, Cameron heard raised voices, tinged with anger.

"You just can't waltz in here and rewrite the rules of Manna to suit your own purpose. You had no right to allow unauthorized people in here."

"Ilsa, if they hadn't been here, we wouldn't have been able to serve the evening meal. There weren't enough volunteers."

Cameron recognized Summer's voice. He pushed open the door and said, "Excuse me." Neither of the women saw or heard him.

Summer's hair was pulled up and back with clips. She wore one of the Common Ground aprons over slacks and a short-sleeve top and had a wooden spoon in one hand. The other woman was in her mid-to late-forties with blond hair cut into a short and severe bob. While Summer was dressed to work, the other woman wore a suit he guessed was both linen and designer.

"Are you implying that I'm not doing my job?" the woman demanded of Summer.

"I'm not implying anything," Summer said. "What I'm saying is that Wednesday is our busiest day. If it hadn't been for Chief Jackson and his men stepping in when they did, we would have had crackers to serve to our guests."

Hearing his name in the middle of the fray brought Cameron up short. Was she being reprimanded for having him work in the kitchen?

From the way she gripped the wooden spoon,

Cameron knew that she was holding on to her temper. Another woman would have been ready to use the utensil as a weapon.

"Excuse me," he said, much louder this time.

Both women turned toward the voice.

"Cameron!" Summer said.

"Who are you?" the suited woman demanded.

Cameron came forward. Summer may have been holding on to her patience, but he was quickly losing his. The accusatory tone of the woman's voice put him on the defensive.

"My name is Cameron Jackson. I'm the Cedar Springs fire chief."

"Oh," the woman said turning on both a smile and the charm. "Mrs. Davidson didn't tell me I had an appointment. What can I do for you, Chief Jackson?"

He glanced at Summer, who looked as if she wanted to be anywhere but there.

"You can tell me why you're berating this woman whose only fault was looking out for the best interests of the homeless and indigent."

"Cameron," Summer began. "You don't have to…"

He held up a hand even as the woman said, "I beg your pardon?"

"*I* was the unauthorized volunteer yesterday," he said. "I dropped off some food donations from the fire houses and discovered that the ladies here were shorthanded."

"Oh," the woman said, glancing at Summer and then turning her attention back to Cameron. "I didn't realize…" she said as her voice faded away.

Then, "I'm sorry," she told Summer, the apology curt and in Cameron's estimation, not at all sincere. "I didn't know that the city's fire chief was the volunteer. That's perfectly acceptable," she said, once again ignoring Summer and giving Cameron a one-hundred-watt smile.

"By the way," she said offering her hand. "I'm Ilsa Keller, the director of Manna."

"Hmm," was Cameron's only response as he gave her a handshake that was at best perfunctory and at worst as abrupt as she had been with Summer.

"Well," Ilsa said. "I have a meeting to attend to. The Women's Club is considering taking Manna on as a service project."

Summer's mouth dropped open.

"My shift is ending," she said. "Who's going to do prep for tomorrow?"

Ilsa shrugged. "Don't worry about it. The work will get done. Chief Jackson, it was a delight meeting you. I hope our paths cross again."

A moment later, Ilsa was out the door Cameron had come in.

"Is it safe to venture out now?" a voice asked from behind a door.

Cameron turned and saw a woman's head peeking out of what he guessed was a pantry.

Summer sighed and put the wooden spoon in the sink. "Yes, it's safe. She's gone."

"Thank goodness. I was getting some raisins for the spoon bread when I heard her come in. Sorry to have abandoned you, Summer. But frankly, I thought staying in the pantry was a better idea."

"That's okay, Olivia. Olivia Green, this is Chief Cameron Jackson," Summer said, making the introductions.

He nodded toward Olivia. "Ms. Green."

"What just happened here?" Cameron said, his issue with Summer's background forgotten as he stewed over the way she had been treated.

"You just saw the Wicked Witch of the West in action," Olivia said, depositing the large canister of raisins on a counter. "She blows in here like that all the time. Never does a lick of work but is always acting like the place would cease to exist without her at the helm."

"Olivia," Summer said. "Be kind."

"That woman doesn't deserve any kindness. And frankly, I'm sick of it," Olivia said. "I've already sent a letter to the board about what's been going on here."

"What's been going on?" Cameron asked as he watched Olivia toss ingredients into a large mixing bowl.

"Summer has been keeping us up and running, that's what's going on. If anybody here deserved a salary for all the work they put into Manna, it would be Summer, not Ilsa."

Summer rubbed her temples. "It's not that bad, Cameron. Really."

"No," Olivia snapped. "It's worse."

"Thank you for coming to my defense," she told Cameron. "You didn't have to. I was already telling her about us being shorthanded here. I just don't think she realizes that the day-to-day operation of this place needs attention just as much as fund-raising and community awareness."

Cameron looked around. "Is it just the two of you or is someone else hiding in the pantry?"

"Summer is leaving," Olivia said. "She's already been here for six hours of a three-hour shift."

"I'm not leaving you when there's…"

"What can I do to help?" Cameron interjected.

The two women glanced at each other. "We *could* use another set of hands," Olivia pointed out. "Especially since Madame Director clearly isn't lending any tangible support."

A few minutes later, Cameron's hands were washed, an apron was tied at his waist and he was chopping vegetables. If he was going at it a bit more aggressively than either Summer or Olivia would have, neither woman said anything about it.

"Does she always interact with volunteers like that?" he asked.

"What you saw is what we get," Olivia said.

Cameron looked to Summer, who reluctantly nodded.

"This is a ministry," she said. "But there are internal, er, issues, that make it difficult to carry out our mission sometimes."

"There's just one issue," Olivia piped up from where she worked. "And its name is Ilsa Keller."

The three made fast work of completing the preparations for the next day's meal service. By the time they finished, Cameron's assessment of Summer had changed...again.

"Can I buy you two a cup of coffee?" he said.

"None for me," Olivia answered. "I have work waiting for me at home. You two go on. I'll wrap up the rest of this. It'll only take me a few minutes."

Summer paused, but Olivia made a shooing motion with her hands. "Go."

Summer surveyed the kitchen. Everything apparently met with her satisfaction because she nodded and headed outside.

"I didn't mean to go all caveman," Cameron said.

"You didn't. At least not that I saw."

The edges of his mouth quirked up. "That's because I kept it inside."

"Those carrots and that celery might disagree."

That earned a laugh. "I thought I was showing off my Iron Chef skills."

"If that makes you feel better," she retorted.

"All right," he said. "I confess. I was letting off the steam that your director brought to a boiling point."

"Twice now you've bailed me out at Manna. Thank you."

Remembering his reason for seeking her out in the first place, Cameron felt a twinge of conscience. His ex-wife would not have been as gracious as Summer, either with Ilsa Keller or with him butting in.

"Cameron, I forgot to ask. What did you come to Manna for? I'm sure your original intent wasn't to referee a fight or to chop vegetables."

To Cameron, her attempt at self-deprecating humor fell a little flat. He'd seen her mouth tremble as she'd fought back the urge to cry after the undeserved dressing down by that woman.

Before he could answer, a horn tooted and they both turned toward the sound.

"Summer Darling! I thought that was you. I heard you were back in town. We still do doubles at the club Saturday mornings. You know you have an open invitation. We'd love to see you."

"I'll call you," she called out to the man who tooted his horn again and waved.

Doubles at the club. Cameron didn't know if they were talking about tennis, golf or something else. But whatever it was, he knew he didn't have an open invitation or even a membership at the exclusive country club.

When she turned back to him, Summer looked troubled.

"Cameron, about tomorrow...."

"That's what I came to see you about."

"I'm sorry," she said. "You've been very kind. But I'm going to have to back out. I'm sorry."

Her words couldn't have been any more shocking. She'd dumped him before he could dump her!

But the snub had the opposite affect on him. Instead of being relieved to have escaped another potential situation like the one with his ex-wife, he suddenly had something to prove—to himself and to Summer.

"I got cold feet," Summer told her sister. "One minute, I was anticipating a date with him and in the next, it was like, 'I can't do this.'"

Spring was finishing up her own volunteer shift at the free clinic run by the Common Ground ministries. Summer had left Cameron standing in front of Manna and gone straight to the clinic. Spring had always been her sounding board, and tonight was no exception.

"And I hate coming across as the damsel in distress," Summer said. "He probably thinks I'm some sort of flake."

"You don't," Spring assured her as she slipped off her stethoscope then shrugged out of the white lab jacket she wore at the clinic. She hung it in her locker, scooped up her bag and faced her little sister. "This is an occasion that begs for ice cream. Let's go."

Ice cream must have been the solution of the evening. When they reached the Main Street shop, Two Scoops & More was packed with people.

And right in the middle of it all stood Cameron Jackson.

Chapter Seven

"Uh, let's go somewhere else," Summer said.

But Spring had spotted the fire chief, as well, and nudged Summer into the crowded ice cream shop.

"Face your fears, little sis."

Cameron had clearly spotted them and was making his way toward the sisters.

As if sensing his urgency, the throng seemed to open a path for him. Summer turned to retreat, but Spring stopped her.

Summer took a deep breath and braced herself.

Cameron wasted no time getting to the point. "Can you at least tell me why you changed your mind?"

"I just did," she said, knowing the answer was lame.

Telling her sister the truth was one thing. She couldn't admit to this man that the reason she didn't want to go out with him was because he made her nervous. Because even though her husband was dead, going on a date with another man felt like cheating.

It all sounded crazy, even to her own ears.

He'd been kind and considerate at Manna, but her gut was twisted in knots, much like the hot pretzels offered in the ice cream parlor.

"I hope you'll reconsider," Cameron said. "Tomorrow is the downtown merchants' Street Stroll. The Main Street stores are all open late. I thought you might enjoy seeing the new downtown."

Summer bit her lower lip. She'd seen an ad about the Street Stroll in the newspaper and was planning to come anyway. It sounded like fun. She turned to get Spring's assessment, but the physician was nowhere in sight. Spring had pulled a disappearing act on her.

"Are you looking for someone?" Cameron asked.

"My sister Spring."

"She left a moment ago. She waved as I was making my way over to you."

"Of course she did," Summer muttered to herself.

It wouldn't be like a *date* date, she told herself. They would be outside and around lots of other people. Sort of like right now. She could handle that much better than the prospect of an intimate dinner date.

The other day when she'd told Spring that she didn't like confrontation, it had been true. She knew the situation with Ilsa Keller was getting out of control. She needed to do something. And then, before she could take the first step in making things better at Manna, Cameron had witnessed her humiliation. There really was no other way to describe that scene in the kitchen. She'd wanted the floor to open up and swallow her when she realized Cameron was standing there seeing the way Ilsa ran the place.

She'd considered leaving, like so many of the other Manna volunteers. But she believed in the soup kitchen's mission and truly enjoyed the work. The only thing that marred it from being a perfect experience was Ilsa…and Cameron seeing her as someone who needed rescuing.

Summer had spent her entire life being cloistered, first by her parents and then by her husband.

"The stroll only comes around once a month," Cameron said, "so the timing couldn't be better. Say you'll come. Please."

Summer's gaze connected with the blue of Cameron's eyes.

Suddenly all of the East Coast's butterflies were having a convention in her stomach.

She dipped a toe into the water and gave a small shiver.

"All right."

The next evening came quickly for Summer. She took extra care with her clothes and makeup, keeping both simple. A strapless sundress and sandals that had heels but were comfortable for walking— or in the case of this date, strolling—was capped off with a fragrance that was light and easy, summery just like her name.

Cameron was prompt. Her front doorbell rang five minutes before he said he'd pick her up.

When he made no effort to come inside, she tucked her house keys in her bag and placed the thin strap of it over her shoulders.

She engaged the alarm system and moments later found herself not in a Ford pickup truck, but rather the luxurious front seat of a Lexus sedan.

Strike one for stereotypes, she thought.

"Why are you smiling?" Cameron asked as he buckled himself in and then started the engine.

"I pegged you as a pickup-truck kind of guy."

Cameron grinned. "I drive trucks and SUVs for the job. I want to be comfortable after hours. Would you like me to go get one of the fire trucks? I could put a helmet on your head and you could hang on to the back of the ladder truck."

She laughed at his teasing. "This is just fine," she said, settling into the luxurious leather.

She did not add what she had been thinking— that even though his vehicle was unexpected, it suited him. He handled it well. That made her a little nervous.

What if he liked to race?

Don't borrow trouble, Summer. And stop thinking about Garrett.

She forced herself to relax.

The drive downtown from her house wasn't long,

but it was long enough to need to fill the time with conversation. People liked to talk about themselves, so before he could ask her any questions, she posed one of him.

"What drew you to firefighting?"

He glanced over at her and grinned. "Probably the same gene that made me get certified in CPR when I was nine or so. Randy, my younger brother, wanted to take swimming lessons. I was worried about him and talked my mom into letting me do the CPR training. I was the youngest person in the class."

He made a sound, sort of like a question.

"What?" Summer asked.

"I was just thinking about what it was that specifically drew me to fire science. It's not like there was a big fire in our neighborhood or anything that really stands out. Like a lot of little boys, I liked the trucks, was enamored with the sirens, the uniforms." He shrugged. "But like I said, most little boys are. With me, it stuck. It was just what I seemed destined to do." A smile followed that pronouncement.

"I also had an incredible mentor," he told her. "Mickey Flynn is one of the best. Not just North Carolina, but the entire country. He spent years in departments, worked his way up the ranks and eventually started teaching master's courses at the academy where I was enrolled. He's been an inspiration to me my entire career. He was the first to explain to me that callings from the Lord weren't just to preach in a pulpit or evangelize on a street corner."

"He sounds like a great guy."

"He is." Cameron's smile carried a wistfulness that Summer interpreted as respect for his friend. "He's going through a rough period right now."

"What's wrong?"

Cameron hesitated for a moment. Then said, "He's fighting cancer. But if ever there was a fighter, Mickey is it. He's gonna come through."

"I'll keep him in my prayers," Summer said.

He glanced over at her, then simply said, "Thank you."

They were quiet for a bit after that. Cameron then turned the conversation to her.

"What about you?" he asked. "Who were the childhood mentors for you?"

"My mom," Summer said without hesitation. "She and my grandmother were amazing women. Gram went to be with the Lord many years ago. She and my mother are women of powerful faith who taught all four of us Christian values, how to love, honor and respect each other and…" she said, drawing the word out for dramatic effect, "how to bake a mean chocolate chip cookie."

That earned a chuckle from Cameron. "Well, I thank your mother and grandmother for that."

Then, "I'm glad you changed your mind," Cameron said as they turned into the downtown district.

"I know this isn't the type of date you're probably used to. But I thought it would be fun."

The Street Stroll in downtown Cedar Springs was an occasion for merchants to stay open late. The extended shopping hours coupled with a free outdoor concert on the library's lawn guaranteed crowds on the warm summer evening. Special deals drew bargain hunters and those who just wanted to get a bit of fresh air.

Cameron parked the car in a municipal lot. He slipped his hand into Summer's as if holding hands while walking down Main Street was normal for both of them.

With a start that gave her a moment's pause, Summer realized it *was* normal. For other people.

But for her, the intimacy of holding hands seemed too much too soon. Without being obvious about it, she freed her hand from his by reaching for a Street Stroll brochure in one of the corner stands.

A lot of residents were out and about, and the atmosphere was festive.

Main Street lived up to its name, serving as a centerpiece for Cedar Springs. In addition to places that existed in Summer's youth, like Mercer's Hardware and the quilting and fabric shop where she'd spent many hours picking out fabrics for doll clothes, there were all sorts of new places including restaurants, specialty shops and even a few art galleries.

"You're right about Main Street changing," she

said as they passed a small internet café. "When I was growing up, there were a few shops bookended by the library and City Hall, but nothing like this. It looks like a lovely little village."

"Exactly," Cameron said. "Cedar Springs has really gone through something of a renaissance. The grocery store that used to be on Main Street moved out to the Commerce Plaza with other big-box retailers. That was a couple of years ago," Cameron said. "With more and more people moving here from Raleigh and Fayetteville, it's almost like a suburb of those cities."

Summer smiled. "A small town with a city vibe."

"Exactly."

"But not really so small anymore," she said. "I read in the paper that the crime rate has gone up."

"That's one of the downsides that comes with growth," Cameron said. "We've seen some residual problems in law enforcement and emergency management. On the fire side, we've had some unsolved arsons. And there's a task force that's been looking into a few things that we think might be linked to organized crime."

"Organized crime? In Cedar Springs?" Summer said with a little laugh. "I've been gone for a little while, but not *that* long. There's nothing here to attract that sort of activity."

Cameron gave her a sidelong look. "Exactly."

"Howdy, Chief Cam," a man said as he passed

by. He tipped his hat to Summer, who smiled. "Evening, ma'am."

"Good evening," she replied.

Cameron said hello and as they continued their stroll, Summer observed. "You won't find that in the big city."

He smiled. "You've got me there."

"The downtown revitalization program has worked so well that city planners are looking at some other areas to replicate the design," he said. "They're bringing in an architect and community planner who's going to present his findings, and then the planning commission will make its recommendations."

"Those recommendations will undoubtedly be to the detriment of town history and property owners."

He looked at her askance. "What would make you think that?"

"My sister, Spring—the doctor—is into historic preservation and isn't at all happy with what she's seen so far. The plans roll straight through our property."

"No site has been selected," Cameron said. "The architect hasn't even made a preliminary design. There will be plenty of public meetings for residents to give input. Only after all of the sites and designs have been studied will the City Council vote. It's far from a done deal."

"That's not what I hear," Summer said. "And I read in the Gazette that Mayor Howell seems particularly keen on getting this project pushed through, no matter what."

"There are a lot of rumors going around, but rumors aren't fact," Cameron said as they passed a young family. The father was holding a curly haired toddler while the mother pushed a large and complicated-looking stroller that presumably contained an infant.

"It's been controversial," Cameron said. "But no one disputes the fact that the Main Street revitalization effort worked. Five years ago, downtown was practically a ghost town. Now it's a vibrant oasis."

Summer paused at a tall pedestal display featuring a curious statue.

"Those are paper clips and bolts," she said pointing to the figurine on the pedestal.

With a hand at her back, Cameron steered her inside the nearby art gallery, its double doors open to entice strollers to consider a look-see.

"Good evening," a woman in a black dress, black tights and high-heeled black boots greeted them. "Welcome to Object d'Art. My name is Allison. Let me know if there's anything you'd like additional information on."

She handed each of them a double-sided placard. "All of our artists specialize in reclaimed or recycled materials."

"I noticed the bolts and paperclip piece outside," Summer said.

The art gallery assistant told them with a smile.

"The artist scavenged the site after the old Piggly Wiggly was torn down."

"Is it all contemporary art?" Summer asked, as Cameron went to inspect a large collage hanging on a wall.

"For the most part."

Summer thanked the woman and then joined Cameron in looking at the artwork. As they were leaving, Allison invited them to the opening of a new exhibit. She gave each of them a little card and a chocolate truffle in a lacy paper cup.

"Please, if you don't take them, I'll eat them all. I got them at Sweetings this morning and there are three left."

"Thanks," Cameron said, accepting the treat.

They ventured back outside to continue their walk. "When did black become the avant-garde and go-to color for the art world?" he asked, as he took her hand.

She glanced down at their clasped hands but didn't say anything or pull back this time.

"It has to do with keeping the focus on the arts," Summer said. "At least that's what I told Winter when she asked that very question when we were in Atlanta a while back. We were attending the gallery opening for one of her friends and in pink, I stuck out like a sore thumb in a sea of black-on-black clothing."

Cameron chuckled. "I'm sure you were beautiful."

Summer glanced at him and smiled shyly. "Thank you."

To deflect the sudden familiarity, she decided to take the conversation in another direction.

"I've never seen you at First Memorial, so I take it you worship at one of the two other Common Ground congregations."

He nodded. "I'm a member of The Fellowship."

"I don't think I've heard of that. Is it a new church in Cedar Springs?"

"Relatively," Cameron said. "Pastor Rick and Theresa Hines started the ministry about five years ago. It began by meeting in a school cafeteria and has grown into a dynamic and diverse congregation of more than eighteen hundred members."

The shock must have been evident on her face. "That's incredible growth for a new congregation. Where are the people coming from?"

"A lot of members of The Fellowship live or work right here in town. Some drive in from Raleigh and Fayetteville. And there is a fairly large contingent that drives in or takes one of the church buses and travel about one hundred miles to get to services."

"Really?"

"Sure. The transportation ministry has an entire fleet of buses and minivans to get people to services and activities, like a car wash that the youth missions team is having. I'm signed up to help out. Want to go wash some cars to help them raise money for an upcoming missions trip?"

She shrugged. "Sure. Sounds like fun and for a good cause. But buses to church? That's dedicated," she said. "I cannot fathom driving that distance to go to a worship service. In Macon, our church was about ten minutes away and that seemed far compared to what I was used to. We all, my sisters and I, I mean, we grew up and were baptized at First Memorial here in town. It was all of a two-minute drive to get to church, five minutes if there was traffic. Sometimes we just walked to Sunday school and would come home after morning worship with Mom or Dad."

"First Memorial Church of Cedar Springs?"

"Yes.

"Hmm," Cameron said.

Before she could ask what that meant, he continued. "The growth of The Fellowship has sort of matched that of Cedar Springs. You know, I never really thought about it in that way," Cameron said. "Hmm."

"What?" Summer asked.

"Just thinking. That makes me wonder if the police chief should have a meeting with the head of the security teams at both The Fellowship and Common Ground."

"Your church has a security team?"

"Congregations of any size should. Even a small church, say one hundred members or so, needs to have someone who is security-conscious. Are the hedges trimmed so intruders can't hide? Is there sufficient lighting in the parking lot? The bigger the congregation, the bigger the potential security issues."

Summer shook her head. "I guess you're right. I just never thought about it. Growing up at First Memorial, there were deacons or trustees who saw to those things."

Summer paused at a trash can to toss away the paper cup from the chocolate treat and to lick her fingers.

"That was good. I'm going to have to check out Sweetings," she said. "This is the third time someone has mentioned the shop."

"The stuff they make should be outlawed," he said tossing his paper cup as well. "It's just that good."

"Well, that's a positive recommendation."

When Summer turned, she let out a small gasp. "What?"

"Look," she said, pointing toward a window display of decorative teapots at the small shop closest to them.

His gaze followed hers. "You're a tea drinker?"

She nodded. "I have a collection of teapots."

"Want to go in?"

She bit her bottom lip, unsure. This was supposed to be a date. But it had been his idea to go on the Street Stroll. Wasn't the whole purpose to go into the shops?

So far this was ranking as one of the oddest dates

she'd ever been on. First a discussion about crime and city management; now she wanted to go shopping.

"You sure you don't mind?"

He glanced at the sign on the window and taking her hand headed toward the door. "There's a Street Stroll special going on. Buy one, get one free."

Summer grinned.

Twenty minutes later, they emerged from the shop, Cameron holding a medium-sized white-and-lavender shopping bag trimmed with lace. It should have looked ridiculous in his hands, but the image of the big man with the dainty bag made Summer smile.

"Promise me I get the first cup from the blend," he said.

"Deal," Summer answered. "It was so nice of her to make that special blend for me."

"I think she recognized a true tea connoisseur walking in the door."

"Well, Tea Time just got a satisfied customer who will be returning," Summer said. She paused and turned to face him. "I really am glad we got together tonight. I was so nervous. I haven't been out on a date in…well, it's been forever. I was a wreck leading up to tonight. And," she said, glancing at the ground for a moment, "the reason I tried to bail yesterday was because I was afraid."

"Afraid? Of what?"

"Dating again. The idea of it."

She decided to keep to herself the part about him making her wary.

"Most women wouldn't admit such a thing."

She gave him a saucy smile. "I, sir, am not most women."

"I got that," he said. "To tell you the truth, I thought you were a lot like my ex-wife and I was thinking about canceling on you."

That stopped Summer in her tracks. She gazed at him open-mouthed, not sure which part surprised her more, the mention of an ex-wife or that he'd wanted bail on the date with her. She also didn't know which revelation stung more.

"I…" She shook her head as if to clear it. Since she'd initially canceled on him, she'd get to that later. "What do I have in common with your ex-wife?"

He shrugged as if it were no big deal. "You're both from wealthy families."

She frowned. "That's pretty generic."

He shrugged again. Summer got the distinct impression that there was more, but he seemed reticent.

"How long have you been…?"

"Divorced?"

She winced as if he'd uttered a profanity.

"I take it there's never been a divorce in the Darling family."

"Well, no. Not to my knowledge. Spring is the

family historian and she'd know for sure. The history dates to the early 1600s...."

"Of course it does," he muttered.

"But I don't know much beyond my great-great-grandparents."

Cameron snorted. "And they were all in the social registry, of course."

She cocked her head. "What's that supposed to mean?"

Cameron shrugged. "You know. Wealthy people keep track of that sort of thing. My guess is there aren't a lot of people in Cedar Springs who can trace their family tree to the fifteenth-century."

Spring had to concede *that* point, but she still didn't like what seemed to be a deliberate snub from him.

"Genealogy is important to a lot of people. And," she added, "for the record, there are several people who can trace their family's roots even further than my family."

Cameron held his hands up, acquiescing to her. "All right, all right. Can we talk about something else?"

"Yes," Summer said. "I'd like to talk about going home. Now."

Later that night, Summer stared at her reflection in the mirror at her vanity table.

They'd managed to avoid the awkward first-date good-night moment at her front door. Because once she got the door unlocked, she'd practically slammed it in his face.

Talk about first-date disasters. If she didn't know better, she would have guessed that Cameron deliberately goaded her tonight. What would have been the purpose, though?

Then a possible reason dawned on her. He was peeved that she'd turned him down twice: first at Manna when he'd asked her to dinner, and then yesterday when she'd backed out of their date. She'd only agreed to the Street Stroll date because she'd planned to go anyway.

She should have trusted her intuition about him. Intuition said run for the hills, but what had she ultimately done? Investigated the valley and gotten caught in the brambles.

Her sisters, she knew, would demand a full accounting of the date. That was something Summer was not looking forward to.

Holding her bare hands before her, she studied them, and then again her reflection in the mirror.

The bare ring finger on her left hand told a story. But that particular chapter had ended…and not with the happily-ever-after she'd anticipated. The chapter of her life with Garrett had indeed ended, and she'd turned the page on to a new one, literally and figuratively. She was in a new yet familiar place. She had a new house, was making new friends, and there was the opportunity for even more. If she wanted it.

It wouldn't be with Cameron Jackson, though. That she was certain of.

She realized that the fear she'd felt about going out with him had been borne of an innate need to be protected.

Did fear and romance go hand in hand? She didn't recall any fear with Garrett. Yes, there would be moments of trepidation and even some self-doubt in the future. But she needed to continue writing her story. And that meant taking chances, meeting new people. And yes, it meant discovering just who Summer Spencer was these days.

From a small crystal bowl on the vanity she plucked a couple of business cards her mother had given her. On the back of each, in Lovie Darling's flowing script, was the important information about each gentleman. Summer glanced at the one on top. Her mother's notes on Oscar Reveau, Ph.D., M.D., F.A.C.S. included: *35yo. NK. Harvard, PhD. JsHpks, med. Raleigh. Presby.*

It had been years since she'd been subjected to the Deal a Man routine—what Autumn had taken to calling the business cards Lovie seemed to shuffle and hand off to her daughters. But Summer easily deciphered her mother's shorthand. Dr. Reveau was thirty-five years old, had no children, had earned a doctorate from Harvard University and a medical degree from Johns Hopkins University. He lived in Raleigh and went to a Presbyterian church.

Summer sighed.

Curious, though, she flipped over the second card to see what her mother had to say about the radiologist who turned out to be engaged. She just shook her head after a single glance. Lovie had put a star in the corner of her notes about him. That meant he was a real keeper, someone personally vetted by Lovie. *34yo. Duke(3). Gma: Lucy H.* Ah, that explained the star, Summer realized. The radiologist's grandmother was Lucy Hardison, the aunt of one of Lovie's dearest friends. That he'd earned not one but three degrees from a fine North Carolina institution were also points in his favor.

Education and pedigree mattered to her mother.

Garrett had had both, but she hadn't fallen in love with him because of his degrees or his lineage.

Summer flicked both business cards into the small trash basket under the vanity table.

She wondered what Lovie Darling would scribble on the back of one of Cameron Jackson's business cards. Summer's notes on the man would be: *Take charge. Handsome. Strong.*

Infuriating. Arrogant.

Cameron ran a hand through his hair and sighed.

In less than an admirable mood, he tossed a bag of popcorn in the microwave and decided to let something on ESPN take his mind off his regret over the way the evening with Summer had turned out.

It had gotten out of hand when he'd somehow

brought Melanie into the discussion. Exes, religion and politics were first-date taboo topics.

He'd been slouched on the sofa in his living room for close to twenty minutes, the flat screen on the wall telegraphing the action on the field. But Cameron didn't even know who was playing, let alone the score of the ball game. His mind was totally occupied with thoughts of *coulda, woulda, shoulda* with Summer.

He'd reached for the phone twice now, torn between wanting to call or text her and trying to keep his distance.

"Stop fighting it," he muttered.

Sitting up, he put the bag of popcorn on the coffee table and reached for the cell phone and started typing a message to Summer: "Can I have a redo?"

Before he could hit Send, the telephone buzzed. A second later, after answering the call, he jumped up, the message to Summer forgotten.

Another fire. This one at an abandoned house that had recently been condemned.

Cameron was grateful for the distraction.

It was better than the thinking about a woman who would only be trouble, a blonde beauty with cornflower-blue eyes and incredibly soft hands.

Chapter Eight

"**D**id you hear that?"

Summer and Manna volunteer Jocelyn Reynolds were in the kitchen preparing sandwiches for bag lunches while three other volunteers bagged cookies, protein bars and fruit cups Monday morning.

Jocelyn, a longtime volunteer at the soup kitchen, was an African-American woman in her mid-fifties who initially started working at Manna two days a week and in the nursery school at her church, the Chapel of the Groves, two days a week. She said the work gratified her and gave her something to do—besides watching television—during the day, while her husband worked. After he'd retired and was underfoot in the house all day, she maintained her volunteer hours—to keep her sanity, she claimed.

Summer paused, her head cocked as she listened intently.

"Hear what?" Jocelyn asked.

"I thought I heard something," Summer said.

"I thought it was just me," said Jenny Grimsley, a thin brunette who'd just started volunteering at Manna this week.

A Sunday appeal at The Fellowship had yielded an outpouring of donations and volunteers.

Summer knew she had Cameron to thank for that. He'd followed through on letting church officials know about the ever-present need for help at the soup kitchen.

"It came from over there," Jenny added with a nod toward the rear wall.

Summer leaned in that direction, toward the wall near the door where donations were dropped off.

"Shh," she said when she heard the sound again.

Was that mewling?

"Uh, I hate to bring this up," Jocelyn said, "but do we have rats?"

"Rats!" Jenny squealed and dropped a cookie on the floor.

"Shh!" Summer directed to the four other women. "There's the noise again. And no, we have no pests here."

Summer put down the knife she was using to cut the sandwiches before deftly folding them in waxed paper.

Even as she was talking, she took a few tentative steps closer to the wall where the sound seemed to be coming from.

Jocelyn came over and nudged Jenny. "Let's pick

up those crumbs before whatever it is thinks we're leaving it lunch."

Wide-eyed, Jenny did as she was directed.

"There is definitely something in there," Summer said.

"Oh, Lord, have mercy," Jocelyn intoned. Her South Carolina drawl was even more pronounced than usual. "This is straight out of one of those horror movies. Someone or something has been in there watching us all morning and is about to attack."

Summer glanced back at the older woman with a scowl.

"Either you've been watching too much late-night television, Jocelyn, or you've missed your calling as a fiction writer. Your imagination is running wild."

Even though the cookie crumbs were up and in the trash, Jocelyn went to the sink, wet a wad of paper towels and wiped at the floor to make sure no treats were left for crawling or four-legged creatures. Then, she moved to the far side of the prep area.

"I'll just be over here," she said, snatching up a rolling pin and hefting it. "You know they like to kill the black people first in those movies. The serial killer, the creature in the basement or the dinosaur always eats, kills or gets them first."

"Jocelyn, you're not helping," Summer snapped, the first time her voice had ever been raised with anyone at Manna.

One of the other volunteers joined Jocelyn and

took her free hand in a gesture of reassurance. "It'll be all right, Miss Jocelyn. See, Summer's not afraid."

"I didn't mean to yell," Summer called back toward Jocelyn. "I'm just concerned. There is definitely something in that wall. And for the record, Joce, there is neither a serial killer nor a cannibal behind there."

"So you say."

Summer shook her head.

"It sounds like an animal," Jenny said.

Summer hadn't even realized the woman was next to her.

"And a small one," Jenny added. "Maybe a small dog or cat. But how did it get back there?"

Their voices apparently encouraged the thing behind the wall because the mewling grew distinct and then urgent, as if the trapped beast recognized that help was nearby and encouraged them to hurry.

With Jenny at her side, Summer went to the wall, trying to locate the opening the animal slipped through.

"There's no break anywhere," Summer said, pushing aside a rolling cart that held extra baking pans and trays. "It sounds like it's coming from between the walls."

"Is there space between the walls?"

"I have no idea."

"This might be a job for the fire department,"

Jenny said. "They get cats down from trees, so maybe they can get one from behind a wall."

The mention of the fire department sent Summer's thoughts to Cameron. Maybe he would be one of the responders. She tried to remember which station house was closest to Manna at Common Ground. His office, she knew, was in the public safety building and that was adjacent to Fire Station Number One.

"That's a good idea," Summer said. "Call, but don't use 911. Call the non-emergency number."

"This is an emergency," Jocelyn said from her safe position across the room. Then, "You're sure it's a cat?"

"98.5 percent sure," Summer answered.

"Uh-huh," Jocelyn said, not moving. "That 1.5 percent left over still could mean a serial killer."

"No more TV for you, Miss Jocelyn," Summer called. "As a matter of fact, after we rescue this cat we're all headed over to your house to remove every TV from the premises."

Jocelyn chuckled and finally put down the rolling pin.

"Okay," she admitted. "Maybe I let my imagination get the best of me."

"Maybe?"

The cat's mewling intervened.

"Hold on, baby," Summer said. "We're getting some help for you."

A crew of three firefighters arrived within minutes of Jenny's call. The rescuers included a short man with broad shoulders, a tall black man and one with model good looks who seemed familiar. Then Summer remembered. She recognized one of them—was his name Randall or Rob?—from the afternoon Cameron had worked with her at Manna.

"Ladies, what seems to be the trouble?" the short one who seemed to be in charge asked as they came in. Each man was looking around for a fire to fight or an emergency to deal with.

"Is it Rob?" she asked the one she recognized.

"Yes, ma'am," he said. "Good afternoon."

"Thank you for your help the other day."

He smiled. "Not a problem, ma'am."

"Please don't 'ma'am' me," she said. "It's just Summer."

He grinned then. "All right…Summer."

"If the flirting is over," the shorter firefighter said, "we can get to the problem. What exactly is it?"

As if on cue, a pitiful mewling sounded from the wall.

"What was that?" Rob asked.

"You ladies have a cat in the kitchen?" the black guy asked, looking around.

Summer and Jenny pointed at the same time. "In the wall," Summer said. "It's trapped. We have no idea how it got back there, but it wants out."

"Can you get him?" Jenny said.

The three firefighters approached the wall, giving it an inspection similar to the one Summer had done. Then they contemplated their options.

"Miss, how did it get back there? There's no opening, at least not one that we can see."

"That's a mystery we hoped you could solve after you free him," Summer said.

"There's an opening somewhere," Rob said. "Ms. Spencer—I mean, Summer—we're going to have to take down part of this wall to get back there. Is that okay?"

"Oh, dear," Summer said. "That's a call that I can't make. Hold on while I see if Mrs. D can authorize something like that."

"I'm right here," Mrs. Davidson said. "Jocelyn came and told me. I've called Allen Hayes—he's the facilities manager for all of the Common Ground sites. He should be here in a few minutes. He was just over at the rec center."

True to Mrs. D's word, Mr. Hayes arrived soon, and after a consultation with the crew from the Cedar Springs Fire Department, he gave the okay for a partial demolition of the wall.

"We can't leave the thing in there," he said in making the decision.

While the fire crew and Mr. Hayes consulted over how to get the animal out while doing the least amount of damage to the wall, Summer hustled the volunteers to finish up the packing of the bag lunches, which they did in record time.

Twenty minutes later, Jenny Grimsley was sitting on the floor with a tabby kitten in her lap. The orange ball of fur looked none the worse for its adventure behind the wall.

"Got it!" one of the firefighters called.

"What?" Mr. Hayes asked. He'd stayed on to oversee the project.

"I see how he got in," the crew chief said. "There's a slit just wide enough to make a curious cat go exploring. Hey, Malik, go around back. I'll shine a light so we can see the opening on the other side."

"On my way, Jose," he said, pushing open the back door.

"Can I see that?" Mr. Hayes asked. "We'll need to get that fixed when we repair the wall."

While the kitten was a little cutie, Summer's thoughts weren't on the cat. She looked around the kitchen at Manna, wondering how they were going to be able to cook and prepare meals if a major construction project was going on.

She was about to guide Jocelyn and the others to the corner for a quick huddle when the swinging door flung open with a force that could only mean one thing. Their mostly absentee director had arrived.

"Why didn't anyone call me?" Ilsa Keller demanded.

"I'm concerned about these fires," Cameron told his assistant chief. The two were in Cameron's office at the Public Safety Building adjacent to Station House Number One.

They were reviewing a cumulative pile of reports from the three shift commanders when they heard the station get a call out. The sound familiar to both men, neither paid it any attention.

Cameron was focused on the fire reports and didn't at all like the pattern he was seeing. "The one Friday night was the seventh one in an abandoned building," he said. "What do you know?"

"All small," Dave Marsh reported. "And like you said, all in abandoned structures. Sheds, garages. Friday was the first in a house."

"How close are we to identifying a suspect?"

Dave handed him a sheet of paper. "We've got it narrowed to these three."

Cameron studied the names. "What's special about them?"

"All teens. The first two, nineteen and seventeen, are brothers and have rap sheets that include setting fires."

"And the third?"

Dave handed him a photograph of the house in Friday night's fire. "His school ID was found on the premises."

Cameron scowled. "The house was empty. Kids may have been using it as a hangout."

"We know they were, Chief. There was plenty of evidence that it was being used for just that. Beer bottles, candy wrappers, lots of cigarette butts, a mattress and some broken down sofas that look dragged in."

That caught his attention. "Dragged in meaning what?"

"Just that. The rest of the furniture in the house is pretty much broken down, and I don't know what you call it, Victorian or something like that. Those sofas with humps on the backs. Lots of burgundy and frills. Musty stuff. The sofas in the living room were modern, like they'd been dragged in from a curb somewhere."

The fire chief pondered that bit of information for a moment. "Could this last one have been an actual accident? Somebody got careless with a cigarette or a lighter?"

Dave nodded. "That's where the evidence is taking us so far. There's nothing like the other sites. No accelerant. Nothing to indicate it was deliberate like the other fires. And the house itself, very different from the other burns. Somebody tried to put out this fire, but it got out of control fast. Lots of combustible materials in there. We may get some prints off of a small fire extinguisher that was in the living room and near the point of origin."

"Okay. That's good." Cameron glanced at the suspect sheet again. "I think it's time someone had a little chat with the Bradley brothers."

"On it, Chief."

After Dave left his office, Cameron sat at his desk in front of the computer. He had reports to read, but his mind kept straying to Summer Spencer and the way things had ended with her Friday night.

That's when he remembered the unfinished text message.

He plucked his smartphone from the holder, tapped a few keys and there it was: his effort at an apology and the invitation to go out again. He pressed Send before changing his mind.

Summer Spencer was a flame and he was the moth who couldn't stay away.

Cameron thought about sending her flowers, but nixed that notion for two reasons: first, it was over-kill. And then, the last thing he wanted was the town gossiping, which would be sure to happen if he ordered flowers from one of the local florists.

On Sunday he'd briefly considered skipping service at The Fellowship and instead slipping into First Memorial Church. Summer was bound to be there with her family.

The Darlings probably had a pew with their name engraved on it in the sanctuary.

That thought reminded him—again—that he and Summer were from two different worlds. And made him question if he still wanted to see her again.

As usual, Ilsa Keller, the director at Manna, was dressed for socializing instead of for meal prepa-ration or other hard work that needed to be done at the soup kitchen.

"What's going on? I was at the church when

several people said there were fire trucks here," she said.

Hustling toward Summer she immediately spotted Jenny Grimsley standing with the kitten.

"What is an animal doing in here? Don't you know we could be shut down for—" Before she finished that thought, she saw the huge hole in the wall. Her eyes darted about the room, trying to reconcile what she was seeing.

"Summer!"

"I can explain," Summer said.

"I've had just about enough of your explaining," Ilsa said. "There has been nothing but trouble here since you arrived."

"That is not true," Summer said.

"Ilsa, you don't know what—" Jocelyn began.

"Joce, I know you like Summer, but clearly..."

The three firefighters tramped back into the kitchen at that exact moment.

"Summer, it's going to take a bit to get you back to normal," Jose, the crew chief, said. "We can put up some tarp until contractors get in here."

"Contractors!" Ilsa screeched. "Summer, you do not have the authorization to hire contractors. And what happened to that wall?"

Summer closed her eyes for a moment, offering up a super-quick prayer for both patience and circumspection. "Ilsa, if you would stop screaming and jumping to conclusions, we can tell you what happened."

"How dare you speak to me that way. Do you know who I am?"

Summer opened her mouth to answer, but before she could, the short and stocky Allen Hayes appeared behind Malik, the tall black firefighter.

"I know who you are, Ms. Keller," he said. "And I must say, I hadn't put much stock in the reports I've been hearing about Manna. But now I've seen and heard it for myself. You owe Ms. Spencer an apology. Right now. And after that, you and I are going to have a little talk…before I go to the board of trustees."

"But…look at that," Ilsa said, pointing to the hole in the wall, "and at that!" she added, pointing to the kitten in Jenny's arms.

"*I* authorized the demolition," Allen Hayes said.

"Which is what I was trying to tell you," Summer added.

"If it hadn't been for Ms. Spencer," Allen said, "that animal could have died behind that wall there. The smell of a decomposing animal isn't pleasant and this place would have had more than just personnel issues to deal with."

Allen turned toward Summer. "I'm going to get a contractor out here today to start work on this," he said. "That way you won't be too inconvenienced."

"Thank you," Summer said. "I was just standing here trying to figure out what we were going to do."

"Don't fret your pretty head," Mr. Hayes told her. "It's all taken care of.

Summer smiled. She knew every one of her sisters, Spring especially, would have bristled at the patronizing words in his remark. But she knew what he meant and didn't hold a grudge.

When he turned back to Ilsa, his demeanor was not at all pleasant. "I'd like a word with you in the dining room. Now."

The volunteers and the fire fighters exchanged the sort of glances that school kids did when the school bully was finally in trouble with the principal.

"Wow," Jose said as the director and the facilities manager disappeared. "She's a piece of work."

"I hope this ends with you running this place," Jocelyn said. "The only reason I haven't quit is that she's never here. I'm just glad Mr. Hayes finally witnessed it."

Summer had been thinking the same thing.

She blinked several times, trying to stem the flood of tears that threatened to fall.

She wouldn't cry. Not now. Maybe when she got home, but not now. Not now.

Jocelyn was at her side a moment later and pressed a paper towel into her hand. "You've got right on your side, Summer," the older woman said. "Just remember that."

Summer nodded and sniffled. "I'm still coming to take those TVs out of your house."

Chapter Nine

Later that afternoon, Cameron looked up when his assistant softly knocked on the closed door of the fire department's conference room.

His brow furrowed at the interruption, but he waved her in. The meeting with his division and battalion chiefs was one everyone could see in the glass conference room commonly called The Fishbowl. And it was one that generally was not disturbed.

"So sorry," Shannon apologized to the group at large as she slipped in.

She made her way around the large table and handed Cameron a note. She took a step back, giving him a bit of privacy as he read it and awaiting his response.

He turned in his seat to look up at her. "I'm on my way," he said.

"Yes, sir." She hustled from the room.

Pushing his chair back, Cameron gathered up his

papers and his portfolio. "Excuse me. Dave, please carry on," he told the assistant fire chief of department operations. "I…I need to go deal with a… a personal matter."

The men and women at the table glanced at each other and then at their boss.

"Chief, is there anything we can help with?" Dave asked.

At the door, Cameron paused, closed his eyes for a moment, then shook his head.

"No. Not really," he said. "But thank you. Dave, brief me when I return."

"Will do, Chief."

Cameron knew his uncharacteristic behavior would be cause for speculation, especially given his vague comment about a personal matter. But he didn't care. He hadn't realized that he'd crumpled the note until he paused at his assistant's desk.

"Did they say anything else, Shannon?"

She shook her head in the negative. "No, Chief. I'm sorry. Just that he'd taken a turn for the worse, was being transported to Duke University Medical Center and that you were being summoned."

Cameron nodded. "I'm headed to Durham," he said. "Would you please reschedule anything I have on the calendar?"

"Already done, sir" she said with a smile and her usual efficiency. "Just one meeting with the deputy mayor about the development project, and Gloria said she was about to call me and see if it could be moved to next week."

"Good," Cameron said absently as he fished his keys out of his pocket and made strides toward the door.

"Chief Jackson?" Shannon called after him.

He glanced back at her.

"I'll be praying."

The corners of his mouth lifted. "Thank you, Shannon. Me, too."

If traffic wasn't too bad, he knew he could get to Durham in about forty minutes. Though he was driving his personal vehicle, he had emergency lights in the Lexus and could easily cut down on the time by playing his fire chief card.

Cameron tossed his gear bag into the trunk and then slipped behind the wheel. He paused to pray, even in the midst of his angst.

"Lord, he needs You now more than ever...."

Cameron Jackson was a praying man, but at a time like this, he found that words failed him.

He made good time in regular traffic and without abusing his special privileges as an emergency manager. He dashed into the large medical complex in Durham, and a few minutes later he'd managed to navigate the halls until he found the right area. Now he paced a family waiting room, alternating prayer with anxious glances at the hallway. A television tuned to a soap opera flickered on mute in one corner.

The walls, a subdued olive with flecks of gold, matched the sofa and chairs—seating that Cameron ignored in favor of the pacing.

"Mr. Jackson?"

Cameron whirled at the greeting. "Yes! Doctor, how is he?"

The two men shook hands. "I'm Doctor Nappon," the physician said. "We have him stabilized. He's asking to see you. But please, make it quick. I can give you five minutes, but no more."

"I'll take it," Cameron said. "Thank you."

He followed the doctor into the intensive care unit.

There, on a bed surrounded by machines and tubes and the devices designed to prolong life, was the man who'd meant so much to Cameron for much of his life.

"Mickey?"

"Hey, looka there. It's Chief Cam." The words, Mickey Flynn's typical greeting for his protégé, were the same, but the voice was considerably dimmed from the usual booming of the big Irishman. The robust heartiness that Flynn was known for had been replaced, and in its stead was the rasp of someone who was gravely ill.

Seeing Flynn like this tore at Cameron. But he masked his anxiety, knowing that the last thing

Flynn would want was pity and the last thing he would need was someone hovering over him looking anxious and worried.

Cameron played the moment the way all of the moments before had been played in all the years he'd known Flynn.

"They called me out of a division chiefs meeting to come up here," Cameron told his mentor and friend. "You always were one for drama."

Mickey grinned, but to Cameron, it looked more like a grimace.

"That's the Irish in me," Mickey said.

A coughing spell followed those words.

Cameron took his friend's hand. Mickey's skin was cool, and his hand thin like the body it now belonged to. Both were a marked contrast to the Mickey Flynn he'd always been. Over the course of his battle with cancer, he'd lost more than seventy pounds.

"Cameron?"

His name came out like a wheeze.

"Yeah, Mickey," Cameron said leaning closer. "I'm here."

"Favor."

Cameron understood the word to be the question it was.

"Anything, Mick. Name it."

"Pray," the older man rasped.

Cameron squeezed his friend's hand, then nodded. He bowed his head. "Okay, Mickey. Let's pray."

* * *

Much later that evening, long after the evening meal had been served at Manna and while the contractors were working their overnight magic in Manna's kitchen, Summer gave in to the pent-up emotions she'd maintained tight control over during the day.

She brewed a cup of tea from the specialty blend she'd picked up while out with Cameron.

The thought of the fire chief coupled with the stress of the confrontation with Ilsa got to her. The tears she'd refused to shed at Manna now flowed in the privacy of her own home. The tea, forgotten, over-steeped in the teapot as Summer sank into one of the chaises in the dayroom off the kitchen.

Despite Summer's brave words while at Manna, the time had come for her to find another way to serve the community. She couldn't, wouldn't allow Ilsa or anyone else to run roughshod over her.

As for Chief Cameron Jackson, it looked as if their little…whatever it was had run its course, as well.

Except for her it hadn't quite dissipated, even after their exchange of words.

Her heart did a totally unexpected little flip when Jenny had suggested calling the fire department this morning.

Summer's first thought hadn't been about the poor, defenseless animal trapped behind the wall, but on whether or not she'd get to see Cameron. It had been, she realized, a foolish hope. It was one thing for the fire chief to go out on new resident calls. That was a perfectly logical and understandable use of the chief's time. Getting to know new people in Cedar Springs was probably part of his job as a public servant. She doubted, however, that he went out on regular calls like putting out fires or rescuing stranded kittens.

Some part of her thought—hoped!—that he would contact her today. Even if all it was was a text message saying hello.

She considered texting him. But what would she say?

Summer figured she had probably broken some cardinal dating rule that everyone knew about except her. It had been a long time since she'd had to navigate those choppy waters.

Things *were* happening between them—things she had not yet fully explored.

Chicken.

Yep. She was afraid. Afraid to explore the emotions that swirled around her regarding the handsome fire chief. Afraid of what the future might hold for her. Afraid that if she lost the work at Manna that she loved so much, she would have no focus in her life.

Things were moving fast, as least as far as Summer was concerned. Garrett had pursued her for months before she'd even agreed to go out with him. Dr. Garrett Spencer had taken it slow even after that. He hadn't attempted to kiss her until their third date.

Cameron hadn't called to apologize for his churlish behavior. She'd half expected to come home to find flowers waiting for her. That's what Garrett would have done.

What if Cameron felt that he had nothing to be sorry about?

Was he waiting for *her* to apologize?

Well, *that* wasn't going to happen.

Her eyes dry now as she worked up a healthy dose of righteous indignation, she got up and paced her kitchen. Before she even realized she was doing it, she'd pulled eggs out of the refrigerator, flour, sugar and baking powder from the pantry and within minutes had a full-scale baking operation under way.

Summer did what she always did when she got stressed. She baked. The act of kneading dough or whipping eggs until they were frothy or putting dollops of cookie dough on baking sheets relaxed her.

Garrett used to say that the only reason he wasn't a four-hundred-pound surgeon was because he maintained a rigorous exercise schedule. The thought of Garrett made her smile, but when she closed her eyes, she didn't see Garrett's face in her mind. She saw the handsome fire chief of Cedar Springs.

At some point in the middle of her second—or maybe it was the third—batch of cookies, Summer had sufficiently calmed down, and a brilliant idea emerged on what to do regarding the Manna situation.

She would have to wait until the morning to make an appointment with Ilsa Keller. She could put into action the second part of her middle-of-the-night baking inspiration after a few hours of sleep.

A phone call to Fire Station Number One gave her the information she needed when she rose. Today was perfect because she wasn't scheduled to work at Manna. She ran a few quick errands to pick up the things she needed then spent the rest of the morning cooking.

When she arrived at the fire station, she had a moment of trepidation. She wondered how her gesture would be received. But the uneasiness dissipated when she walked into the firehouse.

Chapter Ten

"Hey, everybody, look," Malik called out. "It's Ms. Spencer from over at Manna. How's that cat?"

"It's doing just fine, Malik," she said. "It was love at first sight for Jenny. She named him Crevice. And something tells me that's going to be the most spoiled cat in all of Cedar Springs."

"I'm still trying to figure out how it got in there in the first place," he said. "The hole didn't seem big enough."

"Never underestimate the power of a living creature to do what it must for survival," Summer said.

"That's for sure," the firefighter said. "What can we do for you?"

"Nothing," Summer said, hefting the large wicker basket she carried. The basket's handle was tied with a cheerful blue-and-white gingham ribbon. "I brought a little thank you for everyone," she said. "There's more in the trunk of my car if someone can help me. I made chili."

"Chili!"

Suddenly three additional firefighters, all dressed in white T-shirts emblazoned with the fire department's logo, jeans and boots, were at her side.

Summer laughed. "I hope I made enough. And I guess that means you're good with lunch and dessert."

"You betcha! Thanks, Ms. Spencer."

A few minutes later they were all set up in the fire station's mess hall with Summer ladling out chili to the full crew of eight settled around a long trestle table.

"I know summertime isn't really chili weather," she said, "but something about a firehouse and chili seemed to go together."

"And cornbread," Jose, the short firefighter who'd come out to Manna at Common Ground, said.

"You got that right," Malik said. "Don't tell my grandma, Ms. Summer, but this cornbread is better than hers. I know for sure I haven't had food this good since I left her house."

"Yeah, we know," Jose said. "We have to suffer through your sorry excuse for dinner when it's your turn to make chow. We all wish your grandma was here to cook for you."

Malik grinned at Summer. "And lucky for me, and for you, today was my turn to cook. Thank you, Ms. Spencer."

Summer's big pot of chili was plenty and she'd made several pans of slightly sweet cornbread with the recipe her mother used, which had been handed down from her grandmother. The cookies, her own specialty, were double chocolate chip. As far as Summer was concerned, there were fewer things more all-American than chocolate chip cookies and firefighters. And doing something nice for these men made her feel a little better about the way things ended at Manna yesterday.

Laughter rang around the table. As they shared the meal, the chatter along the long trestle table was companionable and boisterous. When someone slipped up and let out a profane word, he quickly apologized to Summer.

She didn't miss a beat.

"Apology accepted," she said. "And I think you owe me a canned good for Manna at Common Ground."

Whoops and guffaws greeted that pronouncement.

"Make him pay up with three or four!"

"Yeah!" someone else concurred amid playful elbow-shoving and extra helpings of chili.

When Cameron walked into the empty station, sounds from the mess hall drew him. Lunchtime.

He'd spent the night in Durham, catching a nap in the waiting room at the medical center and checking in on Mickey whenever he could convince the duty nurse that he wouldn't disturb the patient. Driving against the early-morning traffic out of Durham, he'd made good time getting back to Cedar Springs. He got a couple of hours of shut-eye, then showered, shaved and headed to work.

But he needed a few minutes to get himself composed. The everyday sounds of a working firehouse were the sounds Mickey probably would never hear again.

Mickey Flynn was a firefighter's firefighter. And Cameron knew that if God willed it, healing would and could happen. There was, however, the doctor's prognosis. If Mickey managed to get out of the hospital this time, he'd be headed not home but to a hospice center.

It wasn't fair. And that wasn't his first complaint to God about Mickey.

Intellectually, he knew that fairness had nothing to do with the progressive cancer that ravaged his friend and mentor's body. The remission that had them both so hopeful had been all too brief, just a temporary reprieve. Spiritually, he knew that Mickey was a child of God and that his future in the Kingdom of God was secure. Emotionally, however, it was a different story for Cameron.

He ran a hand across his face and then sighed.

Maybe work would get his mind off the things he had no control over. This was his day to work a shift along with the crew at Station Number One.

Fire chiefs in localities the size of Cedar Springs were usually administrators, long removed from the business of actively fighting fires and going on calls. But Cameron liked keeping his hand in active-duty firefighting and spent one shift each month at each of the fire stations.

Suddenly, he heard a woman's laughter from upstairs.

Cameron's brow furrowed even as his gut clenched. That wasn't his assistant Shannon, and from what he remembered of the schedule he'd glanced at, there were no women on this shift today. Besides, the laughter sounded like it belonged to Summer Spencer. There was no reason she would be at a fire station, let alone whooping it up with his crews.

She hadn't responded to his text message and that irked him.

Loud guffaws and more feminine laughter drifted down. That definitely was Summer Spencer in his fire station.

He took the stairs two at a time and the scene that greeted him drew Cameron up short.

There, as if she belonged in the company of his rough-house first shift crew, was indeed Summer. With her head thrown back laughing at something either Malik or Jose was saying.

Cameron's gut clenched again, this time jealousy hitting him full force.

"Well, looks like you all are having a jolly good time."

The two rookies at the table jumped up at the

sound of the fire chief's voice and stood at attention. The others just turned.

"At ease," he told the rookies, who glanced nervously at each other. "The rest of you should take a few lessons from the neophytes."

Several gave him a salute and turned back to their lunch.

Cameron shook his head. To the two rookies, he said, "Sit. Finish your meal."

"Hey, look who's back," one of the veterans called out, standing up and going for a straight-backed chair to add to the table for the fire chief. "And just in time for a great meal. You've got a nose for fires and good food, Chief."

Another firefighter got a bowl, spoon and a couple of napkins and set them on the table in the empty spot. Right next to Summer Spencer.

She turned, a smile blossoming on her face, presumably at the sight of him since he was the only new addition to the room.

The knot of tension in Cameron's stomach eased.

"Hello, Chief Cam."

He noted how easily she used the nickname just about everyone in town called him. Then again, it was either that or call him by his first name, which would signal to the firefighters a familiarity between them.

"Ms. Spencer."

Cameron took the empty seat even while his

men moved down on the trestle bench to give him more room.

She gave him a quizzical look.

"What brings you here today?" he asked, unable to keep the edge out of his voice.

"A thank-you. To the crew," she added. "We had a little incident over at Manna and these gentlemen, Jose, Malik and Rob, came to the rescue."

Alarm covered his face. "There was a fire? Why didn't anyone call…"

"No fire, Chief," Jose said before Cameron could finish.

"There was a cat," Malik said, snickering.

As the crew explained what happened, Summer took Cameron's bowl.

"I can get it," he said.

She waved him down. "I'm already up. And this is my treat. I served everyone, at least for the first go-round. You're on your own for seconds and be-yond."

He got up anyway and joined her at the buffet where a big pot and a napkin-covered basket sat.

"I thought I would have heard from you," he said, keeping his voice low so it didn't carry to the table where the firefighters ate and joshed.

"What would make you think that?"

"Normally there's some sort of acknowledgment when one party asks for a redo."

Summer paused while reaching for the ladle. "What are you talking about? What redo?"

"The text message I sent you. I thought you would have responded, even if just to tell me to beat it."

Summer filled his bowl with chili, cut two large pieces of cornbread and placed them on a small plate. "I never got any message from you, Chief Jackson."

With that, she took the food and went back to the table.

He ran a hand through his hair in frustration.

She placed the bowl and plate at Cameron's place at the table. When she retook her own seat, Cameron noticed that she'd moved several inches away from him.

"A thank-you note didn't seem quite sufficient," she said. "I was off today and I baked last night, so early this morning I called to see when the three who came out to Manna at Common Ground were working again, and when the firefighters usually ate lunch. I thought a more tangible thank-you might be welcome."

"And we all thank you," Jose said.

Cameron tucked into the bowl. After the first spoonful, he rubbed his stomach. "You don't know how much this is appreciated," he told her. "I saw it was Malik's turn to cook. We're all pretty convinced that he should be on that *Worst Cooks in America* show."

"Hey, I resent that!"

The laughter returned to the table at Malik's remark.

"So who got custody of the cat?" Cameron asked.

"Jenny Grimsley. She's a new volunteer for Manna at Common Ground."

"You all are going to be in steady need of new volunteers if that lady talks to everybody the way she was going on yesterday," Jose said.

Cameron's spoon paused in midair. "What was that?"

Jose and Malik filled him in on the incident at Manna.

"I don't believe this," Cameron muttered. "That woman is a menace."

"That's not a kind thing to say," Summer said.

"But it's true," Malik said. "But Ms. Spencer stood her ground, and that Allen Hayes gave that lady what for."

"Maybe I need to…" Cameron began.

"Gentlemen," Summer interjected. "*All* of you," she added with a pointed look at Cameron. "I'm the one who will be handling this situation. I don't need any of you to run interference. Okay?"

Cameron nodded, but didn't look happy about it.

"It all ended happily," Summer said. "Crevice has a new owner and the kitchen ended up with a new paint job."

"Crevice?"

"That's where he was found. The name fit. The

poor thing didn't have a collar or anything," Summer told Cameron. "Jenny took it to a vet who said there wasn't a microchip, either. The vet checked him out, deemed it a physically fit kitten despite his ordeal and suddenly Jenny has a new kitten to spoil."

"How long is it going to take to get the kitchen repaired?"

"Already done," Summer said. "I am assured that when I walk in tomorrow morning it'll be to wonder if the kitten-in-the-wall incident ever even happened."

Cameron nodded. "Allen Hayes has an army of volunteers on call and contractors on retainer to handle all of the facilities or maintenance issues that crop up at the Common Ground sites."

Conversation flowed around the table for a few additional minutes. Then Summer got up. A moment later she returned to the fire station crew with the wicker basket in hand.

"Anyone save room for dessert?"

Not too much later, Cameron and Summer stood outside near her silver Mercedes-Benz with the Georgia license plate. It featured a hummingbird fluttering at two flowers and was in support of wildlife.

"You need to get that taken care of," he said nodding toward the license plate.

"The personalized tag is on the way. I'm sorry to have to say farewell to my hummingbird, though."

"What did you get?"

"The eagle that says 'In God We Trust.' I liked the message. Thanks for helping me carry things."

"It was an excuse to get you alone," Cameron said. "Summer, I don't know what happened to the message I sent you. I've been kind of distracted. I was up in Durham visiting with Mickey."

"How is he?"

Cameron shook his head. "Okay when I left to come back this morning. But it's kind of touch and go. He has good days and bad ones."

She touched his arm. "I'm sorry."

He nodded. Then, "And I owe you an apology," he said. "About the other day. I unfairly labeled you with a broad brushstroke."

"Your ex-wife?"

He nodded again. "Can we rewind? I do believe that there's some missing ice cream that I owe you."

"I aim to collect," she said.

He smiled. "Good. How about tonight?"

He held his breath, waiting for her response.

Summer tapped her chin and then cocked her head—drawing out the suspense, whether deliberately or just because she really was weighing her options, he didn't know.

"I think that sounds like a date," she said. "But you have to promise me one thing."

"What's that?"

"I fight my own battles. I don't need a champion hopping in and saving me from every little slight or harsh word."

"What I saw, and what the guys described, is more than a little slight."

She cocked her head and folded her arms.

"All right," he said raising a hand as if swearing to a pledge. "If we happen to run into the Wicked…"

She raised a brow and he backtracked.

"If we happen to run into Ms. Keller, I'll retreat."

"Thank you."

"And I'll pick you up at six-thirty," he said. Then, as Summer was about to step into the car he called her name.

She turned back toward him. "Yes?"

He smiled at her, then scuffed his shoe on the ground for a moment before meeting her gaze. "Thanks for giving me another chance. I'm really looking forward to seeing you again."

Chapter Eleven

None of the nervousness that preceded her first date with Cameron plagued Summer this time. She thought it might be because of that hint of vulnerability she'd seen in him. At her car earlier, he'd almost seemed like a teen asking a girl out for the first time. If there was any uncertainty on her part, she attributed it to anticipation. She dressed casual, in walking shorts, a lime-green off-the-shoulder top and espadrilles. Dangling earrings with seashells and a small cross-body handbag completed the outfit.

When Cameron picked her up at her house, he too, was dressed for comfort. Jeans, sneakers and a plaid button-down shirt with the sleeves rolled up to his elbows.

They claimed a booth at Two Scoops & More after placing orders for hot fudge sundaes.

"So, why did you move home to Cedar Springs?" Cameron asked her.

"It was a pretty easy decision," Summer said. "My family was here. Garrett, my husband, his practice was established in Macon. We actually met in South Carolina. My mother has a home there and he was visiting friends." She paused. "Sorry, I'm rambling."

"No, you're not," Cameron assured her. "I'd like to know. Especially since I'm glad you decided to return to Cedar Springs."

"Really?"

"Really. Despite all evidence to the contrary the other day."

She studied him for a moment and then smiled.

"It was time for a change," she said, finally answering his question. "Past time actually. I needed a new beginning. Of course, some of my friends in Macon said, 'Well, if you're going to have a new beginning, why are you going to small-town North Carolina?' They all thought I should go to Atlanta or Charleston. I actually gave Atlanta some thought. It's a city big enough to get lost in. But I missed my sisters. We've always been close. Texting and Facebook isn't the same. Even talking on Skype isn't the same as being able to hug someone. You know?"

He smiled. "Yes, I know."

When their sundaes were put before them, Summer and Cameron enjoyed companionable silence for a few moments as they dug into the ice cream.

"The house you bought is a good one," he said. "It's been well cared for and has good bones."

"Funny you mention the house," Summer said, licking chocolate fudge off her spoon. "That was my big independent move."

"Buying a house?"

She nodded. "I put the house in Georgia on the market. It sold much faster than I would have anticipated, especially given the way the market has been. I took the quick sale as a confirmation from the Lord that the move I planned was ordered in His steps. And then I found the house here on Hummingbird Lane. Even the street name seemed like a sign from the Lord. You saw that there was a hummingbird on my old license plate. The street was cheerful, and the house seemed to say, 'Summer, I'm yours. Buy me.' So I did. It's just the right size. Not a McMansion. Not a historic place that needs a lot of care. It's just a nice house on a nice street in a nice neighborhood."

Cameron plucked the cherry from his sundae and held it out for Summer.

She didn't hesitate in claiming the bite. But she knew the blush that grew up her cheeks as their gazes met probably told Cameron that the intimacy of eating from his fingers hadn't been lost on her.

"So why was buying a place considered an independent move? You needed a place to live after all."

Summer laughed and wiped her mouth with her napkin. "You've obviously not crossed paths with my mother. Lovie Darling is a force to be reckoned with. She—and for that matter, even my sisters—assumed I would move back to The Compound."

"Your family has a compound? Like the Kennedy family and the Bushes?"

Summer waved a dismissive hand. "Nowhere near that scale," she said. "And The Compound is just what my sisters and I have called it. It's really just a big house with additions and some land."

"Some land? Do you mean like an acre or two, or a couple of thousand acres? There are lots of undeveloped parcels on the outskirts of town."

"Well, a lot of land not too far away," Summer clarified. "More than two and far less than a couple of thousand acres, I would imagine. And an old farmhouse. I always loved it there more than the house at The Compound. Many years ago it was actually a working farm. That was before I was born. Spring claims to remember, but the rest of us think she just has vivid imaginings from hearing our parents talk about it. That's the land that the city wants to gobble up for that new development."

Cameron sighed.

"This is clearly a topic that we're going to disagree on," she said. Before he could say anything, she lifted a hand. "Let's just, for now, talk about something else."

He regarded her quietly for a moment before nodding in agreement. "All right, then," he said. "What are you going to do about Ilsa Keller?"

She narrowed her eyes for a moment, not sure

if he was deliberately goading her or if he really wanted to know. Then Summer smiled sweetly.

"Did every conversation with your ex-wife include verbal fencing?"

His mouth twitched. He raised his water glass to her in a salute. "Touché, Ms. Spencer. So, where are you in the lineup of the Darling sisters?"

"Next to last," Summer said, visibly relaxing again since the conversation had headed into territory that didn't have land mines scattered across it. "Spring is the oldest, and hence the bossiest. She was born in the spring and got her name that way. When Winter came along, I think the parents thought it would be cute to have Spring and Winter as daughters. When I popped out as a girl, they were on a roll. And Autumn, who as Mom likes to say, arrived in the autumn of her life, was practically destined to have that name. It would have been a boy's name if the fourth and last Darling offspring had been male. The whole thing is really kind of embarrassing."

"No," Cameron said. "It's actually quite endearing."

Hearing him say that made Summer's heart flutter. She didn't know what to make of that reaction. She ran hot and cold with Cameron. And this was one of those hot times.

The moment passed in an awkward silence as they finished up their sundaes. The arrival of their check gave Summer a moment to gather herself.

Cameron settled it, then rose and held his hand out to her to assist her from the booth.

His hand was large and warm, and Summer enjoyed the security of the small embrace. She liked holding his hand.

"How did you come to Cedar Springs?" she asked him as they headed to his car.

On the drive back to her house, Cameron told her about his career moves, working in small towns and then larger ones until he'd done a military stint; then, after his service, getting into fire administration.

Summer told him about how she chose her house, the help she'd gotten from her sisters and her mother, and what she hoped to eventually do with the rest of her yard.

Before either of them noticed, it was well after nine. They'd been sitting at the curb in front of her house talking for more than an hour.

"I should have invited you in," Summer said.

"This was more fun," Cameron answered before coming around the side to open her door for her.

Hand-in-hand they walked to her front door.

Summer pulled out her keys, unlocked and pushed open the front door, but she didn't move to go inside.

"Thank you, Cameron," she said. "It's been a lovely evening."

He took her hands in his and pressed a kiss to the top of hers.

"Good night, sweet Summer."

She watched him walk back to the Lexus before finally going inside and closing the portal.

Long after she'd heard his car start and pull away, Summer still leaned against her front door.

She was smiling.

After their ice cream date, they ended up talking several times over the course of the week, twice on the phone, and once after going to the new exhibition opening at the Object d'Art gallery downtown.

They carefully avoided the topics that seemed to spark debate between them.

Tonight they'd actually had a full meal together— dinner—and neither seemed willing to head to the movie they'd planned to see.

Summer picked at a thread on the edge of her white linen napkin. "So what about the Jackson family? You haven't told me anything about your family. Do you have siblings?"

He nodded. "Two. A sister and a brother. My sister…"

Cameron was interrupted by their waiter. "Would either of you care for dessert? We have a luscious deep chocolate Bavarian cream pie tonight. It comes with fresh strawberries."

Cameron lifted a brow in question at Summer who was unfolding her napkin and placing it back in her lap.

"I think that that's a yes," he said, grinning at her.

"But we'll split it," Summer said. "And can we have extra strawberries?"

Their waiter smiled. "Coming right up."

"Something tells me I won't be getting many strawberries," Cameron said.

"I'll admit, they're my favorite," she said. "Strawberries are a summer fruit—I think that's why I love them so much. It's like they grow just to celebrate my name." She took a sip of water from her goblet, then placed it back on the table. "You were saying you have a sister and a brother."

He nodded. "Both younger."

"I figured that," Summer said, almost to herself.

"Why?"

"Why what?"

"You said you'd guessed I was the eldest child," Cameron clarified.

"Oh," she said. "That's because you're a protector. Protectors are generally first-born."

He considered her for a moment. Then just said, "Hmm," before reaching for his own water goblet. "My sister is still in Tennessee. My brother is in Alaska now. I think."

"Alaska. Wow, that's a long way from Tennessee. What does he do there?"

Cameron frowned. "Supposedly he works for the forestry service. Mandy—that's Amanda, my sister—has long harbored the conviction that Randy is a CIA agent. He's constantly on the move and always very vague about just what it is he's doing."

"Randy and Mandy. Twins?" she asked.

Cameron shook his head. "Nope. Amanda is named for our grandmother."

She smiled. "Finish telling me about your brother and sister."

Instead, he put his chin in his hand and smiled back.

"What?" Summer asked.

"You."

"What about me?"

"You are absolutely enchanting, Summer Spencer. I don't think I've ever met a woman quite like you."

"I'm sure you have," she said. "Starting with your ex. You've never told me about her."

Cameron winced and sat back. "Can we talk…"

"No," Summer said. "We can't talk about something else. We've been skipping the hard parts, the Cedar Springs development project, Ilsa at Manna and your ex-wife."

"I'll make a deal with you."

Her mouth twitched up. "Of course you will, Chief Cam."

"I'll tell you about Melanie if you'll hear me out on why a mixed-use development would be good for Cedar Springs."

She made a face, but her curiosity about his ex-wife compelled her to accept the deal.

"All right," she said. But before he could begin, their waiter appeared with a large slice of chocolate

Bavarian cream pie surrounded by what looked like a full pint of sliced strawberries.

Cameron and Summer each chuckled.

"Well, I might get a strawberry or two, after all," he said.

The waiter placed a fork before each of them, then slipped away.

Cameron picked up his fork, slid it into the creamy dessert and offered the bite to her.

She accepted it, smiling.

"Mmm," she said. "This is good."

He handed her the fork and picked up his own for a taste, spearing a slice of strawberry along with it.

They enjoyed the dessert in silence for a few moments, their eyes frequently connecting.

"Your ex?" she prompted.

He sighed. "Melanie's parents were—are—quite prominent. They own and operate a company that owns malls and theater complexes all up and down the East Coast.

"She never wanted for anything," he said, "until she married a firefighter who couldn't keep her in the style to which she felt an entitled right. What I made in a month, she spent on a single handbag or pair of shoes. We were young, and we thought that love was all we needed." Cameron snorted. "As long as love comes with a Black Card from American Express."

"How long were you together?"

"On paper, two years. In truth, eighteen months.

She moved out of our apartment and back to her parents' house while I was on a twenty-four-hour shift. The divorce petition came from one of her father's lawyers not long afterward. We both walked away, hopefully wiser for the experience."

"Cameron, I'm not Melanie."

"I know."

"What you said about my mother's house makes sense now."

His brow furrowed. "What did I say?"

"You asked if it was as big as the Kennedy Compound."

"Oh. Yeah. I forgot about that."

"I didn't." She couldn't keep the hurt out of her voice.

"I'm beyond that now," Cameron said.

"Hmm," she said.

"Hey, that's my line."

She grinned. "Now you see how it feels."

Cameron speared a strawberry, held it tantalizingly toward Summer and just as she reached for it, he popped it into his own mouth.

She laughed at his antics.

"Gotta make sure I get a few," he said around chews.

"When I asked for extra strawberries, I didn't mean for them to give us a whole bushel of them."

They exchanged small talk as they made inroads into the dessert, comparing books read and favorite musical artists. They discovered they had much in common, and Summer said she was looking forward to finding a book discussion group to join.

"I miss the one in Macon already. It was from the women's Bible study group at church. We read a variety of books."

"I have to admit, I've never been to a book discussion group," he said, "but I know there's at least one at The Fellowship."

"I think I'd like to check it out," she said.

Cameron then invited her to Sunday service with him.

Summer gave him a smile as bright as that afternoon's summer sun. "I thought you'd never ask."

"I'm glad you changed your mind about going out with me," Cameron said, turning the moment serious again. "I've enjoyed our time together."

"Me, too," she said. "Although, I have to confess, in the beginning, I was a total nervous wreck."

"Really? I couldn't tell," he said. "You are the epitome of cool, calm and grace."

She smiled. "I like that image, even if it's a façade."

"Ready to go?" Cameron asked.

She nodded. He settled their bill and they left the restaurant.

The warm North Carolina evening smelled of summer and the air moved in languid swirls. The humidity had not yet morphed into the unbearable molasses it would be in a month or so.

"It's a nice evening for a walk," Cameron observed.

"It is," she said. "And we can work off some of that rich pie."

In a smooth move, Cameron shifted to the outside of the sidewalk as they began to stroll. Summer smiled.

"My chivalrous knight."

"I grew up old school," he said. "Some habits are hard to break."

"I did, too," she said as she tucked her arm into his. "I fear I am more of a throwback to a bygone era. Our choices of college majors even said a lot about that. My sisters and I, I mean."

Cameron smiled. "What did you major in? No, wait, let me guess. Home economics?"

She batted his arm. "Not *that* much of a throwback, silly."

"That wasn't a silly guess," he mock complained. "Don't forget, I've had your cookies and your cheesecake. Not to mention some awesome cornbread and chili. So if not Home Ec, maybe culinary arts or maybe you were a liberal arts major."

"You get points for deductive reasoning," she conceded. "Spring majored in biology, with a premed emphasis, of course. Winter has an economics degree and a master's degree in business administration. Overachievers those two," she said with a smile in her voice. "Autumn, who has always been the tomboy of the family, got a degree in fitness and nutrition. Three sisters, three practical college careers. And then there was me."

"Who majored in something that made her happy."

Surprised, she turned toward him. "Yes. I was an art history major. Which qualified me to do absolutely nothing."

"That is not true," Cameron said. "It taught you to appreciate art and creativity, even if it comes in the form of paperclips and bolts."

Summer grinned.

"You've taken me out to dinner," she said. "It's my turn to return the favor. I make a mean pot roast. Will you come tomorrow night?"

Before he could answer, his cell phone rang. "Excuse me," he said reaching for it. "That ring tone is the hospital."

Summer studied him while he took the call.

They'd gotten to know each other tonight. And one of the things she'd learned about him made her wary. Her family was well-to-do, and had been for several generations. Based on his description of his ex-wife and her family, their wealth was in another league altogether. But because there were platinum credit cards in all of the Darling wallets, she feared Cameron lumped them all in together.

She saw him end the call and pocket the phone. "How is Mickey?"

"I need to go up to Durham," he said in answer, his voice flat.

"Would you like some company for the drive?"

Chapter Twelve

With Summer beside him, the forty-minute drive to Durham seemed to fly by. He thought it might be the conversation, but knew it was the woman who filled the car and his senses with the fragrance of peaches and sunshine.

"You told me about Melanie," Summer said, "so I guess I have to keep my side of the bargain and listen to your arguments for a land grab."

"We're talking opposition to a project that hasn't even been voted on, and even if it were, it would still be years in the making."

"It sounds like there's a lot to consider."

"There is," he said. "And nothing, pro, con or otherwise, is happening overnight."

They rode in companionable silence for a few miles. Finally, Summer said, "Tell me about Mickey. How and when did you meet him?"

"I first met Chief Mickey Flynn—Michael is his given name, but he goes by Mickey—while I was in the fire academy. He was already legendary in the fire service. And he was the graduation speaker for my class.

"What struck me the most about him was his absolute conviction and dedication to the job. For Mickey, working in fire departments was more than a job. It was both a calling and a way of life for him. I connected with that, with him," Cameron said. "Probably because he was the first person who understood when I tried to articulate why I wanted to be a firefighter."

"Michael Flynn," Summer said.

Cameron smiled. "That's right. Michael Sean Flynn. Irish to the core."

"That name sounds familiar," she said. "I just can't place it."

"That's because if you throw a rock in communities with large Irish populations you'll hit a Michael Sean. And Flynn is a pretty common last name."

"What was the call about tonight? If you don't mind me asking," Summer asked.

"I wouldn't have agreed to let you join me if I minded," he said. "He was asking for me. That in itself is unusual. Mickey has been in and out of the hospital for the last year. This time around his condition is guarded. He has good days and bad ones."

Cameron clenched his fist on the steering wheel. "I leave depressed, angry and mad at God every time I come up here."

She reached for his hand and closed hers over it.

Cameron took a deep breath and unclenched the fist. He then threaded his fingers with hers.

"I'm glad you're with me," he said.

She squeezed his hand in response.

"Despite the cheerfulness of the nurses and doctors on the ward, all they can do is keep him comfortable. I'm listed as his next of kin."

"He doesn't have a wife or children?"

Cameron shook his head. "Lifelong bachelor. But to hear him tell it, he was quite the ladies' man in his day."

Summer smiled. "He sounds like a character."

"He is. You'll see," Cameron said as he navigated the patient visitor parking lot of the huge medical facility.

"Tell me about her," Mickey rasped from his bed not long after giving Cam a key and making him promise to access the safe deposit box when the time came.

Cameron stood at the window gazing out at nothing, wondering if he would or could face the end of life with the dignity and good humor that Mickey seemed to embrace it with.

He turned at his friend's odd request.

"Her?"

Mickey tried to raise a hand to wave away the comment, couldn't manage it and settled for a scowl. "I'm dying, Cam. Not dumb."

Cameron smiled. "Far be it from me to ever suggest such a thing."

"You're stalling."

"Her name is Summer Spencer. But she's just a friend, Mick. I… Well, she's not the type I go for these days."

"What? Not breathing?"

"Funny," Cam said.

"Doesn't exactly rate on the beauty meter, huh? That's okay, Cam. Beauty's on the inside."

Cameron grunted. "She's beautiful on the outside, but…"

"But?"

Cameron faced his friend, who was fighting a valiant but losing battle with the cancer. Mickey wanted to see him settled down, but Cam knew giving his friend false hope wasn't going to do either of them any good.

"But she's wealthy, Mick. Very wealthy. She came from money and married money. I've been down that road with Melanie. And I have the scars to prove that the potholes and sinkholes on that particular stretch of road don't warrant a second trip. So don't go getting any ideas. She's just a friend who came up with me, and she's in the waiting room."

"Cam."

Cameron rubbed his eyes.

His heart ached. Witnessing his friend's last days hurt more than he could have imagined. But Mickey faced the end the way he'd lived each and every day of his life: with a gusto that belied whatever ailed him.

Life hadn't always been fair to Mickey Flynn.

The love of his life had married another man. And like he'd told Summer, on all of Mickey's official paperwork, his next of kin was listed as Cameron Jackson.

Through the years, first starting at the academy when he recognized in Cameron a man who would go far up the ranks, and later as they got to know each other outside of work, the friendship had developed. In Cameron, Mickey found the son he never had. They were brothers in the Lord and brothers in firefighting, and Cameron was left wondering if he'd feel as despondent if it were Randy, his own blood brother, slowly dying.

"Get her," came the command from the bed in a voice that almost sounded like the Mickey of old.

Insisting that she didn't want to intrude on their time together, Summer had settled in the waiting room while Cameron went to visit with his friend.

The magazines didn't interest her, and neither did the offerings on the TV. Her thoughts were on what Cameron had said—and not said—about his friend and mentor. Mickey was dying and Cameron was hurting.

Summer understood that. She was glad she'd come with him. She knew firsthand about grief, and sometimes you just needed another person there to help absorb some of the pain.

She prayed for them both, asking the Lord to give each man the strength he needed for the coming days.

"Hey, Summer."

She looked up to see Cameron standing in the doorway of the waiting room. She rose as he came in.

"How is he doing?"

Cameron grinned. "He wants to meet you."

"Me?"

He nodded. "Do you mind?"

"Of course not," she said, picking up her bag. "Lead the way."

As she entered the room, Summer realized she hadn't been in a hospital in many years. Not since her father's illness and death.

The man sitting up in the hospital bed was a big guy. He winced as if in pain and Summer's heart went out to him.

Cameron led her to the bedside and made the introductions.

"Summer Spencer, this is Mickey Flynn, the best firefighter on the planet. Mickey, this is Summer."

The man stared at her, his mouth open.

"Lovie?"

Cameron groaned. "See, I told you he was a ladies' man."

Summer stepped closer, peering at the man who'd lifted his hand toward her. She took it in his.

"You're lovely, like Lovie."

She glanced back at Cameron. "Mickey Flynn. *Michael* Flynn?"

"You…you look just…like someone I used to know."

"You're *him*. I…" She looked between the two men. Cameron seemed confused. Mickey was squeezing her hand. His grip incongruous with a man who was as ill as he was.

"You know each other?" Cameron asked.

Summer placed her other hand on top of Mickey's.

"Lovie," he said.

"Lovie? Isn't that your mother's name?"

"Darling?" Mickey rasped.

"Yes," Summer said. "My maiden name was Darling. My mother is Louvenia."

"Gardner."

Summer gasped. "I knew that name sounded familiar. You're Michael Flynn. *The* Michael Flynn." She turned to Cameron who'd come around to the other side of the hospital bed and was intently studying Mickey.

"Sit," Mickey said. "Tell me. Lovie. How is she?"

He let her hand go long enough for Summer to pull a chair closer to the bed.

"How does he know your mother?" Cameron asked.

Summer saw the exact moment when light dawned on Cameron.

"The one that got away," he said. "Your mother…" He stared at Mickey. "*Her* mother was the one who got away."

Mickey's color was high. He seemed to have recovered from seeing the woman from his past walk into his room looking exactly as she had decades ago. While the four Darling sisters all resembled each other, everyone always said Summer looked most like Lovie did in her younger days.

"When you said your friend's name was Michael Flynn, I couldn't remember why it was familiar," Summer said. "When he called me Lovie, it all fell into place. My mom used to date a Michael Flynn before she met and fell in love with my dad. We all knew about it because it was a part of my parents' story."

Mickey nodded. "She was the only woman I ever loved."

Summer's eyes teared up. "Oh, Mr. Flynn. I'm sorry. I didn't mean…"

"Not your fault," he said. "What was meant to be was meant to be. She found happiness with John, and I was glad that she was happy. And you, you look just like her. Beautiful."

Summer blushed. "Thank you."

A nurse came in then. "Chief Flynn, time for your vitals. If you'd step out for a few minutes," she told Cameron and Summer. "This won't take long."

"All right," Cameron said. "We'll be just outside, Mickey." Then, to the nurse, he said, "His heart rate might be up. He just got a shock."

From his bed, Mickey Flynn grinned.

Cameron guided Summer from the room as the nurse wheeled her cart around.

The door had barely closed behind them when Summer whirled around and was digging in her purse for her phone. "I cannot believe this!"

"I don't think you're supposed to use that here," Cameron said indicating her cell phone.

"Oh, I'm not making a call. I want to show him some pictures of Mom. She's not going to believe this. Michael Flynn. *The* Michael Flynn. My parents' romance was like something out of a fairy tale. We used to love hearing the story. It was so romantic that Dad came in and swept her off her feet."

"While breaking Mickey's heart."

Summer stopped tapping on her phone and cast stricken eyes up at him. "I…I never thought about it from that perspective," she said slowly.

She stared down at the image of her mother, taken just a few weeks ago after church. Lovie was radiant in peach. Summer had liked the picture so much she'd had a print made of it.

"Maybe I shouldn't."

Cameron ran a hand through his hair. "I don't know, Summer. He hasn't been that animated in… well, it seems like forever. May I see it?"

She held out her mobile phone. The woman smiling back at him was, indeed, beautiful. He saw what Summer would look like in thirty years. He could also see what had caught Mickey's eye all those years ago.

The hospital door opened and the nurse came out. "Mr. Jackson, he's asking to see you."

"I'll go to the waiting room," Summer said.

Cameron looked torn, then he nodded. He watched Summer head down the hall, then he headed into the room.

"Wow," Mickey said.

"Well, you look like you're ready to be discharged."

Mickey grinned, and to Cameron it *was* like seeing the pre-cancer Mickey.

"What a wonderful gift," Mickey said. "Provident that it should come now."

Cameron wasn't sure he wanted to know what Mickey meant by that. But he asked anyway.

"I'm not fooling myself, Cam. And neither should you. Despite what you said, and it could be that you don't even know it yourself, but you wouldn't have brought 'just a friend' to see me. I'm on borrowed time. I made peace with that. What about you?"

"What do you mean?"

"Do you love her?"

Cameron ran his hand through his hair again, the gesture one of mute irritation. "Mick, we've been out a couple of times. But love?" He gave a harsh little laugh. "You of all people should know there's no way I'd get seriously entangled with someone like her."

Mickey's snort of disgust turned into a cough. When Cameron moved toward him, Mickey waved him away.

"Listen to you. *Someone like her.* That Melanie did a number on you," he groused. "Don't be like me, Cam. I loved Louvenia Gardner and spent the rest of my life wondering and regretting that I didn't fight harder to keep her. Don't make the same mistake I did. Don't let a good woman get away because you're afraid of getting hurt."

He paused for a moment, either in reflection or to catch his breath, Cameron didn't know which.

And he didn't like the connection Mickey was making between Summer and his ex-wife. The conversation with Summer about Melanie was still too fresh in his mind. Summer had told him she wasn't Melanie, and now he was hearing it from Mickey, too.

"I can't get over how much she looks like her mother."

Cameron made a noise that could have been a grunt.

"Well, there are three more just like her."

Mickey's eyes widened. "Lovie has four daughters?"

Cameron nodded. "I've met all but one of them. But the oldest is a doctor and the family resemblance between her and Summer is unmistakable."

Mickey smiled, apparently liking the idea.

"I wonder what she looks like now. She had blue eyes that I thought I'd drown in and legs that went on forever."

Mickey closed his eyes for a moment, and had what could only be described as a dreamy smile on his face.

"Probably still is as much of a looker as she was back in the day," Mickey murmured.

"She is," Cameron said.

"So you've met the mother," Mickey said without opening his eyes. "Things are progressing. That's good."

Cameron shook his head. "I haven't met Mrs. Darling. Summer has a picture on her phone."

Mickey sat up, apparently too fast because he sucked in his breath and leaned back in the bed.

Cameron rushed to his mentor's side. "Take it easy, Mick."

"Do you think… That picture…"

"I'll go get her," Cameron said as he made sure Mickey was comfortable. "She went back to the waiting room."

A few minutes later he returned with Summer. Her astonishment about Mickey knowing her mother was as profound to witness as Mickey finding out his first love had four daughters.

"Cam tells me that you have a picture of your mother on your phone," Mickey said. "Would you mind…"

Summer was already pulling her cell from her purse. "Of course," she said. "This was just a few Sundays ago after church."

She had lots of photos on her phone, so Mickey looked at images of Summer and her sisters, but he kept returning to the one of Lovie Darling.

Cameron watched his friend as he talked to Summer. And he saw what Summer didn't see: the love shining in Mickey's eyes as he looked at the picture of the woman he'd loved and lost.

Cameron's gaze shifted to Summer.

She was telling him something about Spring, but Cameron was thinking about what Mickey had said. Cameron couldn't help but wonder if he had let his ex-wife color his thinking so much that he'd let someone genuine and true slip away.

"I can't wait to tell Mom about meeting Mr. Flynn," Summer said as they were headed back to Cedar Springs. "What a small, small world it is."

"I take it they didn't keep in touch through the years."

She shook her head. "Not to my knowledge. He seemed to be in really good spirits," she said.

"That was all you," Cameron said.

"What do you mean?"

"There's nothing like a pretty woman to lift a man's spirits, sick or otherwise."

She smiled. "Now who's the flirt?"

"I really am glad you came," Cameron said.

"Me, too. Mom is going to be stunned."

"Do you think she had any regrets?"

Summer gave him a startled glance. "What do you mean?"

"About what could have been. I mean between them, her and Mickey."

"If she did, she never gave any indication of it. She and my Dad were happy together, truly happy. Their marriage taught the four of us what it really meant to love and be loved. They lived and breathed their wedding vows."

Cameron thought about that as they headed home. Summer was the kind of woman a man could love for decades like Mickey had loved her mother. Cam wasn't sure if he had it in him to love a woman like that.

Chapter Thirteen

Summer had a busy day ahead of her, but she could barely contain her excitement as she arrived at her mother's house first thing in the morning. Through the years, Lovie had spoken about Michael Flynn with fondness, and she knew her mother would like to know about him.

When she didn't find Lovie in the kitchen or in her bedroom, she went to the intercom and called out. "Mom, where are you?"

"In the solarium, honey," came Lovie's reply.

Summer shook her head and smiled. *Solarium.* Only Lovie Darling would come up with a name like that for the covered walkway that connected the main house to Spring's space. The addition to the house that had once served as her father's medical practice had been converted into living space that Spring now called home.

"Summer, bring that basket on the island counter."

Making her way through the house, Summer

went to the kitchen and plucked up the small wicker basket her mother used for dried herbs. Lovie grew her own.

A few moments later, she found her mother snipping greenery from the potted plants that practically filled the space.

"It's starting to look like a jungle in here," she observed as she placed the basket near Lovie, who was bent over fresh mint. "Are you trying to completely close off the pathway so Spring can't get through?"

It sure looked like it. What used to be at least a four-foot wide limestone walkway leading from Lovie's kitchen to the mud-room at Spring's place was now a barely discernible path filled with large pots on the floor and on benches. A few spots remained where you could actually just sit amid the natural beauty. Flowers also grew in the space that could better be described as a greenhouse.

"Spring accused me of the same thing," Lovie said, dropping the mint into the basket and then straightening to hug her daughter. "You look lovely today, dear. That color becomes you."

Summer glanced down at the teal sundress. "Thanks," she said. "I have one just like it in a color called 'strawberry lemonade.'"

Lovie grinned. "That sounds like a wonderful idea. Let's go make some." She placed her gloves and the basket on a bench and turned Summer back toward the kitchen. "I got fresh strawberries from Hannaford's just yesterday. Of course, I got too many for just smoothies and dessert, so lemonade is the perfect solution."

As Lovie went about gathering sugar and lemons, Summer pulled out the juicer.

"Mom, you are never going to guess who I met yesterday."

"I hope it was that nice Dr. Reveau. I think the two of you would hit it off marvelously."

Summer bit back a sigh. "No, Mom, it wasn't Dr. Reveau. I met someone from your past."

Lovie opened the refrigerator and pulled out a pint of plump strawberries. "My past?"

Summer nodded. "Your *romantic* past."

Lovie's brow furrowed as she put the berries in a colander and ran cold water over them from the sink in the kitchen island. "I don't have..."

"I met Michael Flynn."

The colander clattered in the sink as it fell from Lovie's hands. She looked as startled and dumbstruck as Mickey had when she walked into his hospital room.

"What did you say?"

"Michael Flynn. I met him last night in Durham."

Lovie's hand went to her chest. "Oh, my," she said bracing the other on the island as if for support. "Oh, my."

Alarmed, Summer went to her side.

"Mom?"

"I'm all right, honey. That's just... Wow. That's a

name I haven't thought about in years. He was such a nice man. I'm afraid I broke his heart."

The strawberries and lemonade forgotten, Lovie motioned Summer to sit in the breakfast nook with her.

"Tell me all about it. How did you happen to meet him?"

While Summer told her mother the story, she didn't realize she'd also revealed her budding relationship with Cameron. It was a fact that didn't escape Lovie.

"So you've been dating this fireman?"

Summer blushed. "Oh, he's the fire chief for the city. And I, well, I wouldn't go so far as to say we're 'dating.'"

She didn't want to talk about Cameron with her mother. She tried to turn Lovie's thoughts back on Mickey Flynn.

"I showed him your picture," she said. "The one from church a few weeks ago. He said you're even more beautiful now than you were then."

A wistful smile played across Lovie's mouth. "Michael always knew the right thing to say."

Lovie took her daughter's hand. Summer was surprised to discover how cold her mother's hand was.

"H-how ill is he, Summer?"

She shook her head. "Cameron said he probably won't leave the hospital. He's got maybe a few weeks left. I'm sorry, Mom."

Lovie blinked back sudden tears. She patted Summer's hand. "Let me go get something to show you."

When she returned a few minutes later, her eyes were decidedly redder than they'd been when she'd left.

Even after all these years, Lovie maintained a soft spot for Michael Flynn. It was sweet. And, Summer thought, incredibly sad.

As she watched Lovie settle back with an old scrapbook in her lap, Summer wondered if there was more to the story about Michael Flynn, Lovie Gardner and John Darling than her parents had ever revealed.

"You okay, Mom?"

Lovie nodded. She swallowed and then invited Summer closer.

"Your father used to tease me about holding on to this," Lovie said, opening the scrapbook, "but I couldn't bear to part with it. I don't believe in throwing away the past just because it's over."

She turned to the first page and for the next hour, she and Summer relived via snapshots, concert ticket stubs and other memorabilia, including a few pressed flowers, the months when Lovie had been Michael Flynn's girl.

The long visit with Mickey had taken a toll on Cameron. He was already tired, and the work day had been interminable. He'd hoped to get home to catch up on some sleep. But it was City Council meeting night, and even on good nights they tended to drag on.

This one was bound to be even longer than usual. At least twenty citizens had signed up in advance to address the council during the public comments portion of the meeting. They typically had three to five people, two of them regulars who liked to admonish the council members and emergency managers about everything from litter to the height of grass in public greenways.

It didn't take a genius to suss out that all of those people were here tonight to oppose the development project.

He hoped Mayor Howell and the other council members had a better argument for the development than he'd presented to Summer. Instead of being reassured by what he said, Cameron got the distinct opinion that her open mind on the issue was taking a turn in another direction.

Neither he nor the police chief were elected officials, but both were expected to be at the City Council meetings every month, available to answer questions from citizens, city staff and the elected representatives on the council.

All he wanted tonight was a couple of extra-strength Tylenol tablets and his bed.

Cameron patted his pocket, looking for the headache medication. He remembered he'd tossed the bottle in his gear bag. A glance at his watch told him he had time to dash out to the car, get it and be back before the invocation and Pledge of Allegiance that opened every City Council meeting.

He retrieved the pills and downed three with a sip of water from the fountain outside the council clerk's office. He was about to head back into the council's chambers when he overheard part of a conversation.

"I just don't understand what she sees in him," a woman was saying. "He's not a doctor."

"Everyone on the planet isn't a doctor, Mom," the answering voice said.

He'd heard *that* voice before. It belonged to Dr. Spring Darling. Were the women talking about him?

"But you know how…" the rest of the words were somehow muffled. "…she hasn't even had him over for Sunday dinner. That says a lot if you ask me. Why is she sneaking around and hiding him?"

So they *were* talking about him! The man Summer was seeing who wasn't a doctor.

Cameron felt a knot in his gut.

Was Summer hiding him from her family?

It figured. She was just like Melanie.

What would ever make him think Summer would be any different than his ex-wife? The two had way more in common with each other than either had in common with him. *Common* being the salient adjective there, he thought with bile rising.

Summer didn't think he was good enough to meet her mother. The woman who'd broken Mickey's heart and married a doctor—just like her daughter had—and just like his ex had left him for.

It wasn't as if he'd taken her home to meet his own mother. But she was in Tennessee, a long way from Cedar Springs. Summer's mother lived across town, all of ten minutes away.

Cameron stared at his hands. He might be the fire chief, but his hands were those of a working man. No, he didn't have a medical degree from an Ivy League school, but he'd put himself through college by working nights and earning his bachelor's degree. He didn't belong to the local country club where Mrs. Darling, no doubt, sat on the board. But he'd knocked down a kitchen fire there his first week on the job.

Summer and her mother apparently considered him the hired help, someone to be hidden away from view.

The headache he'd just taken three Tylenol to combat suddenly throbbed even stronger in his head.

Cameron glanced around the corner. The women were disappearing beyond the doors leading into the City Council chambers. Definitely Spring Darling. And the older woman with her, the one who clearly didn't care much for a working-class firefighter, even a fire chief, dating her precious daughter, could only be the indomitable Lovie Darling.

What had Summer called her mother? *A force to be reckoned with.*

With less than a charitable spirit, Cameron entered the room, took his seat between the police chief and the city manager and stewed.

The tension in the room was already palpable. Residents wanted information about the proposed new development and had come en masse to confront their elected officials.

Since Dr. Spring Darling and her mother were sitting with a few people Cameron recognized from the historical society, he surmised that they were among the opponents to the project.

How could they or anyone else be against a project that hadn't even been presented to the City Council? The architect's presentation to the council hadn't even been formally scheduled.

Cameron focused his attention on the meeting when Mayor Howell started speaking.

"I can appreciate your concern," she said into the microphone at her spot in the middle of the raised platform that held the seven Cedar Springs City Council members' seats. "But at the moment, it is misplaced concern, Georgina."

Cameron knew that Georgina Lundsford was the past president of the Cedar Springs Historical Review Advisory Committee. The historical committee members were well versed on the law and on the historical significance of just about every property within the city limits. Most of the members were also members of, or connected to, the Cedar Springs

Historical Society. The difference between the two groups continued to confound and elude him.

But Bernadette Howell didn't get to be mayor of Cedar Springs by being a shrinking violet. As far as Cameron was concerned, the two women were evenly matched, each believing the other wrong and clearly suspecting a hidden agenda.

As he watched the byplay between the mayor and Mrs. Lundsford—what his mother would call a nice-nasty exchange, unpleasantness disguised in polite words and tones—he became aware of someone watching him. His gaze shifted from the woman at the speaker's podium and across the audience. He saw her then.

Dr. Spring Darling didn't avert her eyes when his gaze connected with hers. She maintained eye contact with him and then mouthed the words, "I'm sorry."

Had she seen him in the hallway?

There was no other reason for Dr. Darling to apologize to him.

Sorry for what?

He raised an eyebrow in silent question.

When her gaze shifted ever so slightly to the left where her mother sat erect in her seat listening to the mayor and Mrs. Lundsford, he knew he'd guessed correctly. She *had* seen him and knew that he'd overheard her mother's harsh words.

As the City Council meeting wore on, he wondered when and how Spring Darling would approach him.

It didn't take long.

The Cedar Springs City Council always took a brief recess after the assorted proclamations and the public comment period and before the start of the evening's formal meeting.

While some people stood and chitchatted among themselves, others got coffee or a soft drink. Cameron usually used the twenty minutes to catch up on email or pulled out his tablet to read the most recent cover story in his fire chiefs' journal. Occasionally a resident would have a question for him.

When he heard the quiet, "Excuse me, Chief Jackson," he figured it was a city resident with a smoke alarm or other fire safety question.

It *was* a resident of Cedar Springs, but he knew this one was not interested in talking about fire safety, or the fire department's budget. She was dressed in cream-colored linen slacks with a blouse and blazer. A large chunky necklace of sand-hued stones and turquoise hung at her neck.

It screamed "I'm wealthy and influential."

Cameron rose. "Dr. Darling. Hello."

She held out a hand, "Call me Spring, please."

He nodded. And then waited.

"Do you have a moment?" she asked after a brief hesitation. "For a personal conversation?"

He nodded. "We can talk over there," he said,

indicating a door leading to an anteroom off the council chambers.

When the door closed behind them, she got right to it.

"This is rather embarrassing," she said. "I know you overheard part of the conversation between me and my mother before the meeting started."

He nodded.

"And taken out of context, it probably sounded very…" she struggled for a word.

"Condescending? Snobbish?"

She winced. "Yes," Spring said. "Both of those things. I'm sorry. It's just that Lovie can be…rather forceful in pursuit of her goals. And she has tunnel vision when it comes to one of those goals."

Cameron remained silent.

"She's of an age where she has a big empty house and no grandkids to fill it with. She wants to spoil grandbabies. And with four daughters, all of whom she considers 'of prime marrying age' and not a single one of us even remotely looking like we'll be marrying any time soon, she's grown impatient.

"She… We," she amended as she tucked her small clutch bag under her arm. "We know you and Summer have been seeing each other, and she wants to know what your intentions are. It's not an excuse," Spring added. "But it is an explanation."

"Hmm," Cameron said.

"Even if Mother doesn't realize it, the rest of

us know the reason Summer hasn't invited you to The Compound."

"Because I don't have M.D. after my name?"

Spring blinked as if startled. Then she shook her head. "No. That's not it at all," she said. "Like any mother, my mother wants what's best for her children, and that's even though all four of us are now grown women all leading active and independent lives. My sister Autumn would say Mother needed a hobby, but she has several and they keep her just as busy as meddling in our business does."

Cameron's lip twitched at that, mostly because he could relate. On more than one occasion his sister Mandy had called complaining about what she considered maternal meddling.

"No," Spring said, shaking her head. "It has nothing to do with you not being a doctor. Not being a doctor probably works in your favor with my sister, although, from what I gather, fire chief sounds like it's probably even more demanding than the hours that doctors put in."

"Speaking from experience, *Doctor* Darling?"

"Touché," she murmured. "Summer hasn't invited you to dinner at The Compound because any dinner or lunch or brunch at the house isn't going to be about the meal. It will be an inquisition, Lovie-style."

"Lovie-style?"

She nodded, and made a slight grimace. "Usually when girls bring boys home, it's the father the boyfriends worry about. Not at our house. When we were growing up and dating, everyone was cool with Daddy. He made them laugh. He gave our boyfriends tips on fishing or cars, recommended them for internships and summer jobs, and if he really liked them, he'd grant an extra half an hour on curfew. It was Mother who made our dates sweat. Big time," Spring said.

"My guess," she continued, "is that Summer is sparing you what would be a most unpleasant, bordering on painful, experience of one of Lovie's meals."

Despite the reason for their conversation, Cameron found that he liked Spring Darling. She didn't flinch from controversy and stood up for what she believed in. He knew she'd inherited that trait from her mother, the indomitable Lovie Darling.

"Thank you, Doctor...." He paused, then amended to say, "Thank you, Spring. Your candor means a lot."

"I just didn't want you to leave tonight with that... With her comments as the first impression you have of her."

When they returned to the City Council chambers, the clerk was bringing the meeting back to order. As they finished with city business, Cameron studied the two blonde women sitting side-by-side. In one he saw Summer ten years from now, and in the other, he saw that she would age into an elegant and striking woman.

He liked what he saw. A lot.

But looks didn't make a relationship.

Despite Spring's admirable defense of her mother, Cameron was all too familiar with how a relationship could and would turn. At first Melanie loved that he was a firefighter, a real-life superhero, she used to say. But the subtle digs had started almost immediately after the honeymoon.

And the honeymoon—partially funded by her parents—was when and where things started going downhill in *that* relationship. Melanie's parents were already aghast that their precious princess was marrying someone who wasn't listed in the social register or on the Forbes list. Princess Melanie—what he'd teasingly called her before realizing that she acted as if she *were* royalty, had never flown commercial in any class except first. The idea of flying coach from Tennessee all the way to Hawaii was abhorrent to his former in-laws. Wanting to keep his new bride happy, he'd accepted the "wedding gift" of first-class round-trip airfare booked just two days before their departure.

Cameron should have realized then that things were going to get bad. The experience with his ex-wife didn't kill him, though. And he knew to beware lest he find himself ensnared in the same type of situation.

When Cameron saw Summer again, he didn't mention the conversation he had with Spring, but they did talk about the big topic of the City Council meeting. Two articles in the Cedar Springs Gazette covered the meeting, one on the proposed development for the city that had the members of the Historical Review Advisory Committee up in arms, and the second article on the other business conducted during the meeting.

Both Lovie Darling and Georgina Lundsford were quoted in opposition of the project. The newspaper's reporter had faithfully recorded the testy exchange between the mayor and Mrs. Lundsford.

"How did your mother's name go from Louvenia to Lovie?" Cameron asked.

Summer's brow furrowed. "You know, I don't know. She even signs her name as Lovie Darling."

They were on their way to a car wash at Commerce Plaza. The Youth Missions Team from The Fellowship was sponsoring the event as a fundraiser for its upcoming mission trip. Cameron had signed up to help wash cars and Summer had remembered his invitation to join him. Since all hands were welcome and needed, Cameron didn't beg off. She had the newspaper open on her lap as Cameron drove.

"Hardly anyone calls her Louvenia. She must have told the reporter her first name, or he—" she glanced down at the article to see who wrote it "—she did some homework. All my life, all I've heard anyone call her is Lovie."

Summer read the article about the development. "Spring is beside herself," she said after she finished. "She's working behind the scenes doing research on land use. When she gets riled up, there's no stopping her. She got that from Mom."

Cameron nodded. "She didn't speak during the public comment period of the council meeting."

Summer shook her head. "She wouldn't. Not yet, at least. She's in the historical society and wants to see the plans first. The tentative date of that public meeting with the presentation to the City Council is marked in big red letters on her wall calendar."

"At least there's someone willing to wait to see what's being proposed. The council members are just as curious and interested in seeing the proposal. What I don't understand," he said, "are all the objections before anyone has seen anything. I've had no less than five calls already from people concerned about the impact on fire and EMT response if there's a new and large residential component to the plans. All development isn't necessarily detrimental just because it's development."

"That's where the advisory committee and the historical society part ways—or so Spring says. I have yet to get a grasp on what's the difference between those groups."

"Tell me about it," he muttered.

"But, Cameron, we don't need to see plans to know it's going to impact us. That's why Mother and Spring were there, to keep tabs on the entire thing. The land the city is considering is adjacent to our property and that's been Darling land for a long,

long time. That's why Spring's title and boundary research is imperative. She suspects a land grab could be in the works."

"Why didn't *you* attend the City Council meeting?"

She scrunched up her nose. "A council meeting with all that gavel banging and motion making is not for me. That's Spring's thing. She's Miss Community Engagement. If she needs me there, I'll be there for moral support. But for the moment, I'm just getting myself acclimated with the community."

"But you're from here," he observed.

Folding the paper, she tucked it between the seats and crossed her legs. "It's different," she explained. "Even though I grew up here, those years were through the eyes of a child and a teenager. I went away to college for four years, only coming home for breaks. Plus, I spent two of those summer breaks abroad. Then I got married. So even though Cedar Springs is home, I'm getting to know it for the first time—through adult eyes."

"I get that," Cameron said. "And what do you think so far about your hometown?"

"I like what it's become," she said with a smile. "Usually when you return to a place after an absence, everything seems smaller than it was in your memory. It's the opposite. There's so much more here now. And in just a few short years. It really is a little city, not so much a small town anymore."

"Progress."

"That's what I hear they call it," she said. "You know, my dad still made house calls. That was into the 1990s. Who still did that?"

Cameron grinned. "Nobody. I thought house calls went out in the fifties and sixties."

"Not in the Cedar Springs I grew up in. Spring says she used to go with him. I don't remember that, but it makes sense given that she was almost ten when I was born."

They passed through downtown Cedar Springs, taking a shortcut to Commerce Plaza via a street parallel to Main.

"I really like the Main Street renaissance," Summer said.

He nodded. "It looks good."

They spent the next two hours with the teenagers from the Fellowship's Youth Missions Team washing cars and interacting with the public. The first ninety minutes flew by in a blur of suds, water and wiping tires, doors and windows of cars, minivans and even a boat that a couple hauled in on a trailer. While the men and the teenage boys washed the vehicles, the females and younger kids brought in business with hand-made signs held high and calls out to drivers entering and exiting the plaza's main entrances.

"Let's go see if we can drum up some more customers back at the intersection," Summer suggested to the car wash cheerleaders.

She and a group of girls gathered up signs that

had been made and raced off together toward the main entrance of the shopping plaza.

Cameron was utilizing the lull to hose off some of the rags used to wash the cars when Joshua Mc-Kinsey, one of the youth team coordinators, joined him to do the same with a pile of sponges.

"Thanks for your help today, Chief Cam, and for the pretty assistant you brought."

"Don't get any ideas," Cameron said.

"I'm not trying to horn in," Joshua quickly added. "Just stating a fact. Besides, anybody with eyes can see that the two of you were meant to be together. She's a born leader with the girls. You think Summer might be interested in being a youth group mentor?"

Although he was a bit younger than Cameron, the two men had become fast friends in ministry at The Fellowship, even though Josh insisted he was not and would never be a minister.

"She's not a member of The Fellowship," Cameron said.

"Really?" Josh said with a tone that could best be described as teasing. "So, if she isn't a member of the church, but she's out here today with you laboring on behalf of the missions team, this is like what, your idea of a date?"

"No," Cameron said. Then, apparently realizing how sharp and almost angry he sounded, he added, "How did *you* get roped into this today? I thought you weren't interested in being co-lead for the Youth Missions Team."

Joshua made a face and shook his head. "Webber's wife conveniently went into labor. Around three in the morning, my phone buzzed and he sounded like he was in the middle of having a heart attack."

Cameron grinned.

"I wished him a happy baby's birthday and resigned myself to the fact that no matter how I try to run, the Lord keeps pulling me back to this group."

"There's a lesson in there," Cameron said.

"Yeah," Josh said with a wry smile. "When the phone rings in the middle of the night, check the caller ID before answering.'"

At the end of their shift at the car wash, Cameron and Summer both gave a monetary donation to the cause, the big bucket already bulging with cash, checks and change. When they were back in his car, he told her about Joshua's suggestion of her working with the youth team.

Summer was quiet for a bit, her brow creased in thought. She pulled from her bag a tube of lip gloss and then flipped down the mirror on the sun visor to apply it. When she finished, she turned toward him.

"Let me think about that. I've never worked with teenagers before."

"The kids on the missions team are a good bunch."

He thought about what Joshua had said regarding Summer's church affiliation.

"I was wondering," he began. "A while ago, you said you'd like to go to a service with me at The Fellowship. How about the upcoming second Sunday? It's Friends and Family Day."

Summer's expression looked ruffled. "Cameron, I'd love to. Really. But I can't," she said. "I have a, well, a family thing."

"Sunday dinner at Mom's?" he casually asked.

"As a matter of fact, yes. My sisters and I go to church with Mom and then have dinner with her every second Sunday."

Cameron waited. As the silence between them in the car wore on, he realized that he was waiting in vain. No invitation to Sunday dinner was forthcoming from Summer.

He was disappointed, but somehow not surprised. Despite what her sister had said, he'd heard Lovie Darling loud and clear outside the council chambers.

He wasn't wanted in the Darling family.

Summer had finally been able to arrange a meeting with Ilsa Keller. It probably wouldn't be a pleasant twenty minutes, but she couldn't see any other resolution to the problem.

The night she'd spent baking cookies for the fire house crews she'd come to the realization that working at Manna wasn't something she needed to do. She enjoyed it, but there were other places and opportunities for community service. She'd realized that during the car wash.

And despite Cameron's distance—there had definitely been an unexplained chill in the air with him when he'd dropped her off—she enjoyed working with the youth group girls today.

Maybe that was why she was actually there. Was the Lord showing her another way to offer service? That had to be it. Common Ground had several outreach ministries. She had no medical skills and would be useless at the free clinic where Spring volunteered. But maybe she could do something at the recreation center or the homeless shelter.

After cleaning up and changing clothes, she checked her messages and found she'd missed a call from Spring.

Summer sank onto the bed after listening to her sister's message about what had transpired at the City Council meeting.

"Well, now his weirdness this afternoon makes sense," she told Spring when she reached her sister. "No wonder Cameron was so cool today. He probably thought we'd already talked and that I knew all about what he'd overheard."

"I tried to reach you," Spring said.

"I know," Summer said. "It's not your fault."

When she got off the phone with Spring, she

knew that the conversation with Ilsa wasn't the only potentially painful one she needed to endure.

She stared at her cell phone for a moment, then sent Cameron a text: We need to talk about my mother.

Chapter Fourteen

The last thing Cameron wanted to talk to Summer about was Lovie Darling. But he agreed to meet her at a coffee shop back at Commerce Plaza.

When he arrived she was sitting at an outside table looking as pretty as summertime. He parked and walked toward her. Like him, she'd changed from the casual shorts, top and flip-flops that she'd worn earlier that day at the car wash, and was in some sort of shift dress with a belt and high-heeled sandals. As his eyes traveled over her, he thought about what Mickey had said about Lovie Darling. Summer had definitely inherited her beauty from her mother.

A delicate gold chain that disappeared under the top of her dress was her only accessory this afternoon. And her hair was pulled back in a ponytail with sunglasses perched on her head.

Cameron was again reminded of the moth and

flame analogy. But he also remembered what Mickey had said about not living to regret something.

"Hi, Summer," he said as he reached the shop's outdoor patio.

"Hey, Cam."

He slipped into one of the wire-woven chairs.

"I ordered us a couple of iced coffees," she said. "I hope that's okay."

He nodded.

"Summer..."

"Cameron..."

They both began at the same time. Cameron yielded.

"I want to apologize about what you heard my mother say."

He shook his head. "Mrs. Darling has champions in her daughters."

"It's my fault," Summer said. "She, well, she's always trying to fix us girls up. That's why I hadn't said anything to her about you...about us. Then when I was telling her about Mickey..."

Cameron nodded as understanding dawned. "I slipped into the conversation and she wondered if I was worthy."

Summer shook her head. "No, she mourned for what was lost with Mickey. She cried, Cameron. I can't remember the last time I saw my mother cry. It had to have been when my father died. She's a very strong woman."

A server brought the iced coffees. Summer took a sip from hers. Cameron didn't touch his.

"Your comment in the car about Sunday dinner makes sense now."

"You talked to Spring." His statement wasn't a question.

She nodded. "There was a message from her when I got home from the car wash." She pushed her iced coffee glass away and leaned in toward him. "Cam, I didn't invite you to Sunday dinner because with my mother, it's always about more than dinner. The meal is just the subtext for..." she paused, trying to find a word "...her none-too-subtle form of interrogation."

"Hmm," he said.

"Don't 'hmm' me, Cameron. Tell me what's on your mind."

He was pretty sure that wasn't a good idea.

"Summer, I'm not interested in going out with your mother. I'm interested in you."

Because I can't seem to help myself, he added silently.

What, exactly, was it about this woman that appealed to him so much?

"Really?"

Those big blue eyes seemed suddenly filled with equal parts wonder and fear, a curious combination that endeared her to him even while part of his brain told him to run for the hills.

He nodded.

Summer smiled. She reached for her iced coffee, took a sip and then sat back still holding the cup. "I've given some thought to what you said earlier today, after the car wash."

"About what?"

"Working with the Youth Mission Team. I'm going to quit working at Manna."

"That's a mistake. I've seen you in action there, Summer. You're a natural. You work well with the volunteers and the guests, people like Sweet Willie and the other homeless people. They need you."

"But Ilsa…"

"Ilsa Keller shouldn't run you out of something that you love doing. From what I've witnessed, she's the problem, not the rest of you who volunteer there."

"I have a meeting coming up with her. I was going to tell her I'm resigning."

"Just give it some more thought," he said. "That's all. Pray about it. Retreat may not be the answer."

She nodded. "What about you? What were you going to say?"

When he'd come out here, his plan was to have her say her piece and then go on his way. So the words that came out of his mouth probably surprised him as much as they did her.

"I was thinking that maybe you'd like to give me another shot."

She eyed him warily, which was what he deserved. "Why?" she asked. "You've made it clear that…"

"I'm an idiot," he said.

That made her laugh. He liked the sound of her laughter.

"Go for a drive with me."

"We just spent the morning together," she pointed out.

"And now it's the afternoon."

She smiled. "All right. Let's go for a drive."

"Have you been out to Fountain Lake Park?" he asked as he slipped behind the wheel of his Lexus after she settled in the passenger seat.

"Not in forever," Summer said. "The last time was probably when I was in Girl Scouts."

"It's a nice drive out there," he said.

"Sounds like a plan."

Summer's shoes were barely made for walking, let alone hiking, so they parked at one of the scenic vistas overlooking the lake that the park was named for. Cameron powered down the windows and cut the engine.

His goal for this outing was to get to know Summer more, avoid the land mines he seemed to always step on when they were together and just enjoy the afternoon in her company. It all went well until the trip back into town.

"So, what was it like growing up in Cedar Springs?"

She shrugged. "I don't know. Normal. With four girls who had wildly different interests, my mother had to figure out how to keep the peace among us. Autumn was only interested in sports, which I took no interest in. Spring could spend hours in the library. I wanted tea parties and dance lessons all the time, and poor Winter, who just wanted to come home from school and talk on the phone with her friends, found herself dragged around from one activity to another."

"You went to public school?"

She cut a glance at him. "Yes, Cameron. My sisters and I are all products of the Cedar Springs Public School system."

"Hmm."

"Is that your little passive-aggressive way of disagreeing with everything?" she asked.

"I may be a lot of things," Cameron said, "but passive aggressive isn't one of them. And there's no need to get your hackles up, Summer. I just thought you were one of the academy girls."

"I did go to the academy," she said. "But not the one you're thinking of. The Augusta Griffin Academy was more hoity-toity than my parents could stand."

By now they were back at Commerce Plaza, and Cameron pulled into the space adjacent to the one where Summer's Mercedes was parked. Neither moved to get out of his car, even after Cameron cut the engine. Sitting there, they continued their conversation.

"So what private academy did you attend? A finishing school in Switzerland?"

Summer was beginning to get more than a little irritated. Cameron Jackson was being rather patronizing and it was irking her.

Did he think she was some spoiled rich girl?

The fact that that's exactly what she was only served to irritate her all the more.

"Are you deliberately picking another fight or is this just a continuation of the one you started the other day?"

He jerked as if she had slapped him.

Summer stared at him for a moment, disgust etched on her face and disappointment clouding her eyes.

"I'm leaving," she said, bending to get her bag.

He halted her with a light arm on hers. "Summer, you told me you spent some summers abroad. I just thought…" He shook his head. "Why are you angry? What just happened here?"

"If you don't know, that's all the more reason for me to leave."

She was out of his sedan before he could get out to open the door for her.

He stood next to his car as she gunned the engine of her Mercedes-Benz and peeled out of the parking lot.

"What just happened here?" he asked the air around him. He got no answer, not that he had really expected one.

Women.

An hour later he was still trying to figure out how a pleasant afternoon had turned into an argument with Summer.

Replaying the conversation in his head, he could not pinpoint where things fell apart, but he knew if he didn't figure it out, his chances of anything developing with Summer were going to be nil.

Summer didn't know what was more frustrating—hearing the subtle put-downs from Cameron or having him not realize that he had a chip on his shoulder the size of a boulder when it came to certain things.

Swiss finishing school, indeed.

She would not apologize for or be made to feel guilty for having money. Her parents had worked very hard to make the comfortable life they offered their daughters, and Summer had fallen in love with Garrett Spencer, not the wealth he'd inherited from his family or earned by working long, exhausting hours in a demanding field.

Summer thought about calling one of her sisters to vent, but they would probably say she was being just overly sensitive—as usual.

At a stoplight, she reached for her cell phone, then she decided on a better option. Making a U-turn, she headed toward the place that always made her feel better.

The old house always felt like coming home.

Although she, like all of her sisters, had a key, Summer didn't go inside. She took off her shoes and settled on the swing on the porch of the farmhouse.

She loved the comfort and the solitude of the porch swing—and what it represented to her: family and good memories.

As far as the eye could see was Darling land. But not for much longer—if her mother agreed to the sale that was being pitched by the developer. None of them harbored any illusions that that developer was somehow connected to the project Mayor Howell was so interested in—the one allegedly in just the preliminary stages of planning.

Lovie had said she wouldn't make a decision without getting independent views from her four daughters, but Summer and her sisters already knew they would agree to whatever their mother wanted.

Money wasn't an object. Lovie Darling had plenty of it—in her own right and inherited after Dr. John Darling's death. Spring's concern about the proposed development was what would be destroyed in the name of progress. Lovie wanted what was best for the town she loved…and for the legacy she would eventually leave her daughters.

Money.

Cameron had plenty of hang-ups about it, whether he wanted to admit to them or not.

Summer had enough on her mind about their

burgeoning relationship without his hurt feelings confusing her even more.

Summer pulled out the gold chain from around her neck. Hanging on the fine herringbone gold was her wedding ring and engagement ring. She'd taken them from the jewelry box and put them on the chain. She needed the reassurance they brought her.

That she'd worn them while out with Cameron hadn't escaped her notice.

"Somehow I thought that would be you driving up."

Summer screamed and nearly fell out of the swing.

"Spring! Do not sneak up on me like that! You practically gave me a heart attack."

Spring Darling stood in the doorway of the farmhouse. She pushed open the screen door that creaked, and carried out two glasses of lemonade. She handed one to her little sister, who glowered at her.

"I thought you heard me coming downstairs."

"Well, I didn't."

Spring raised an eyebrow at the snappish tone, but didn't make a comment. She instead settled on the porch's top step, placing her glass of lemonade on the step below her.

"I came out here to think," she said. "That City Council meeting gave me a headache, and I could barely concentrate at work today. I just took off and came out here. I was taking a nap when I heard you drive up."

"Were those surveyors' flags I saw on the drive to the house?"

"Yes," Spring said, anger tingeing her voice. "I told Mayor Howell that trespassing laws still exist."

Summer took a sip of the tea. "What'd she say?"

"'Spring, dear, no laws were broken.'" Spring said in an exact mimic of the mayor. She then harrumphed, a very un-Spring-like sound. "I've been trying to have an open mind about this whole thing, but what I heard at the council meeting did not sit well with me."

"Or with Mrs. Lundsford. Did you see what she said in the paper?"

Spring nodded as she reached for her glass and sipped the refreshing lemonade.

"I don't want us to lose this house," Summer said.

"Neither do I," Spring said as the sisters quietly took in the pastoral view of green from the porch. Several tall magnolia trees lined the driveway and a riot of perennials bloomed in untended beds in the front yard.

"Mom is worried about you," Spring said after a while.

"I'm worried about me, too," Summer said.

Spring moved her glass out of the way, got up and went to sit next to her sister on the swing. She pushed off with one foot to get them swinging.

"Want to talk about it?"

Summer bit her lip. "Cameron and I just had a fight. I think. He can be so infuriating. He acts like having money is some sort of curse. His ex-wife left him and went back to her uber-wealthy parents."

"His ex-wife?"

Summer's lip curled. "Melanie. Every time I think we're making some progress, establishing a connection that could turn into something more, he says something to push me away. It's like Melanie is sitting on his shoulder poking him. Then he makes these little jabs at me. It's…it's infuriating."

Spring smiled. "Yeah, I got that. Are you in love with him?"

The gentle question startled Summer who fingered her rings and shook her head.

"In love?" Summer parroted. "Now isn't the time to talk about love. What I am is in confusion. I like him, but…"

"But your head and heart are still with Garrett?"

Summer turned stricken eyes toward her sister even as she rubbed the rings again. Spring noticed the gesture, and put an arm around her sister's shoulders.

"He'd want you to be happy, Summer."

"How do you know?"

"Because he loved you."

The Darling sisters sat in silence for a long time, enjoying the quiet company of each other in the warm sun. Summer knew that Spring understood her need for silence, for a contemplation of the day.

After a while, Spring got up and went in the house. She returned with the pitcher of lemonade, topped off their glasses and then quietly asked, "How are you feeling?"

Summer tucked one bare foot under her and reached for one of the throw pillows on the other side of the swing. Clutching it to her, she gave her sister a wan smile.

"A little shaky," she confessed. "Part of me can't believe it's been two years already. I miss him at odd times. Like when I took the car in to be serviced. Garrett always used to tell me, 'Don't let them cheat you.' As if I knew anything about cars. That was his thing."

She gave a little shrug and plucked at the fringe on the pillow's edging.

"And sometimes," she added, "I feel guilty because days or weeks go by and I haven't thought about him."

She held out the rings before dropping the chain. "I think that's why, even after seeing Cameron this morning, I came home and reached for…comfort. Part of me feels like seeing Cam means I'm forgetting Garrett."

"No, it's called moving on," Spring said reaching for and clasping her sister's hand. "There's nothing for you to feel guilty about. As a matter of fact, I think Garrett would like the new Summer."

Summer raised a brow at that. "The new Summer?"

Spring nodded. "The one who laughs and smiles, goes out and embraces life."

Chewing on that thought, Summer remained silent for a few moments.

"I took the car in for servicing this week—oil change, a tune-up, tire rotation, detailing…"

"They must love to see you coming."

That crack earned a small smile.

"…because I wanted to be ready in case I decide to go to Georgia."

"Georgia? For what?"

"I was thinking about going to the cemetery to see him. On the anniversary. To leave flowers or…I don't know."

After a moment, Spring said, "Summer, it's a six-hour drive to Macon."

Summer frowned at her sister in irritation.

"I tell you I'm about to hop in the car and go see my dead husband's grave and your only response is that it takes six hours to get there?" Temper laced her words.

Spring flashed a bright smile that was gone as quickly as it appeared.

"Actually," she said, "that was my fourth response. I edited the first three and verbalized the fourth."

Summer shook her head, the anger gone as quickly as it had come. "She of moderation and diplomacy."

"Two underrated virtues."

"Tell that to Autumn…or better yet, tell Winter,"

Summer said. "So, I want to know, what were those three unspoken first responses?"

"You *really* want to know?"

Summer nodded.

"Well, first up was…" Spring said, ticking off with a lifted finger, "'Have you lost your mind?' Since I didn't think that was quite appropriate, it was quickly followed by, 'I don't think that's a good idea.'"

"And the third?" Summer prompted her.

"Third," Spring said, "was 'Garrett is gone, honey. A trip to his grave site might make you feel better, but are you going there to say goodbye again, or are you running away from what's facing you right here, namely Chief Cameron Jackson?'"

Summer made a face. "Okay, I see why you decided on option number four."

"And?" Spring said.

"And what?"

"And what's the answer to that question?"

Summer tossed the pillow aside, took a sip from her lemonade and placed the glass back in the cup holder built into the arm of the wooden swing.

"Did you give up on pediatrics and switch to psychiatry?"

Spring didn't respond. She sat quietly, waiting for Summer to own up to her feelings. Summer knew the ploy well. Spring had used it before and it was as effective now as it was then.

She sighed. "Sometimes I hate when you do that."

"Do what?" Spring asked, the picture of innocence. "I'm just sitting here enjoying the afternoon and a glass of lemonade with my sister."

"Exactly," Summer said, exasperation making the word sound like a prosecutor nailing a trial witness on a key point. "You're messing with my head." She turned toward Spring then and softly added, "But thank you."

"For?"

"For voicing the very question I've been reluctant to answer myself."

She cast distressed eyes at her older sister. "I like him," she said. "I like him a lot, Spring. That it's been two years since Garrett died seems…" She shrugged. "I don't know. Maybe it seems like I shouldn't be happy."

"'I come that you might have life and have it more abundantly.'"

Summer smiled. "John 10:10. That was one of Garrett's favorite Scriptures." She let out an unladylike snort. "The one he used to justify his little hobby that got him killed. He said he was just living an abundant life."

"And what about you, Summer. Are you living an abundant life?"

Chapter Fifteen

Cameron wished he had a date planned for the evening. But Summer wasn't answering his calls or text messages. It was Wednesday and he'd taken to spending a few hours at Manna at Common Ground. Yes, he did the volunteer work because Summer Spencer was there. But in the weeks that they'd been seeing each other he found he enjoyed the time spent interacting with the people who came to Manna for sustenance.

Specifically people like the homeless man known only as Sweet Willie.

Summer never called him that—she called him Brother Willie—but everyone else had taken to the nickname that the man said he'd been called his entire life.

Although Cameron wasn't sure if Summer would welcome his presence at Manna tonight, he wasn't going to leave the volunteers shorthanded because he'd had a disagreement with her.

"Been seeing a lot of you here these days," Sweet Willie told Cameron. After placing a fresh basket of rolls in the center of the table, Cameron took the empty seat at the end of the table near the elderly black man.

Elderly, Cameron realized, may not have actually been correct. The man was stoop-shouldered but tall, a fact that was evident even while sitting. His brown skin didn't have the wear of time, and his eyes were sharp. Like he was constantly on watch, taking in everything around him.

Most of the older men who ate meals at Manna before shuffling off to the shelter had rheumy eyes or the gloss of cataracts.

"I like giving back to the community," Cameron said.

Sweet Willie chuckled. "I think you like Miz Spencer, too."

Cameron gave a little chuckle.

"That, I do," he admitted. He might not admit it to Mickey or even to himself, but the truth always came out when he talked to this man.

"She's a good woman. And a fine cook. Ain't bad to look at, neither."

That earned an outright laugh from Cameron. "You're right about that, Sweet Willie. Where are you from?" he asked. "Originally, I mean?"

The older man shrugged. "Oh, here and there. Spent some time in Virginia and up in New York.

Had to get outta there, though. Them people crazy." Sweet Willie reached for his coffee mug and glanced at Cameron. "I been noticing a few things around town," he said.

"A few things like what?"

A squabble one table over drew Cameron's attention for a moment. The dispute, between two men over a salt shaker, was resolved when Summer appeared and handed each man a pair of salt and pepper shakers. He smiled.

When Cameron turned his full attention back to Sweet Willie, he found the man regarding him with what seemed to be unwarranted intensity. The gut instinct that Cameron relied on kicked into overdrive. He sat up a little straighter and repeated the question. "A few things around town like what, Willie?"

The man pursed his lips. Cameron waited.

"I'm telling you this," Sweet Willie said, "'cause I been watching you. You're a straight shooter, Chief Cam, and that can't be said 'bout everybody. You need to keep your eyes open."

"Am I looking for something in particular?"

The man looked to his left and then his right as if spies might be eavesdropping on their conversation. Cameron began to wonder if maybe Willie was delusional. He didn't know anything about the man or his background. Just that he showed up for the occasional meal at the soup kitchen.

Cameron knew the statistics on mental illness

among the homeless. Maybe Sweet Willie was one of them. Paranoia and delusional thoughts were common.

His next words dispelled the notion that mental illness was factoring in to the man's actions.

"Things ain't what they seem over on Elmhurst," Sweet Willie murmured.

Hackles rose on Cameron's arms. That was one of three addresses in Cedar Springs that he and the police chief suspected had been targeted by an organized criminal gang from Raleigh. They had no proof and no probable cause, so for now they were, as Sweet Willie said, keeping an eye out.

"What do you know about that street?" he asked the man, his voice as low as Sweet Willie's.

"Not a lot," the old man said. "Just enough to know things ain't right."

Whether the ramblings of a delusional homeless man or the astute observation of someone who spent most of his time on the streets, Cameron could appreciate and respect the man's desire to alert the authorities to something he considered amiss.

Cameron patted the man on the shoulder. "Okay, Willie. I'll take that advice. Will you do me a favor?" he asked, reaching into his back pocket for his wallet. He pulled out a business card. He scribbled a number on the back. "Here's my card," he told the homeless man. "And on the back is my cell number. Twenty-four/seven," he said. "You see any trouble while you're out and about, you call me. Anytime. Any day. Okay?"

The man nodded, accepted the proffered card and tucked it into a pocket on the patched-over jacket he wore despite the warm summer temperature.

"You a good man, Chief Cam. You a good man."

"You be careful out there, Willie."

The old man smiled and Cameron was struck at how much younger Sweet Willie looked when he did so. "Always do."

"Hmm," Summer said shortly before they would bid good-night to the final guests. The dining room was almost cleared out and volunteers would soon be in to clean and prepare the tables for the next meal.

"Isn't that supposed to be my line?" Cameron asked.

"So it is."

"I'm sorry for the other day," he said. "I have some lingering issues I need to work out."

The simple apology was the best he had to offer.

She smiled at him. "Accepted. Just remember, Cameron. I'm not your ex-wife."

"Noted."

"If you're not busy, I'd love for you to come to second Sunday dinner at my mom's."

He raised an eyebrow. "Really?"

She nodded.

"I'd be honored."

"And," she said, "that was a connecting-the-dots 'hmm' from me."

"What dots need to be connected?"

"Vanessa Gerard, one of our longtime volunteers."

"Yes, I know her," Cameron said.

"I saw you talking to Brother Willie earlier, and it reminded me."

"Of?" Cameron prompted.

"She told me she thought Sweet Willie was following her the other night."

Cameron glanced over at the table where he'd been sitting and talking to the man earlier. He was gone now, had probably shuffled off to either the restroom, the homeless shelter or wherever he sought shelter at night.

"Following her where? He has a car?"

"A car? I don't know. Not following her like outside, but watching her. Here at Manna. She said it was kind of intense. Like he wanted to talk to her or warn her about something. But that's crazy," Summer added. "She doesn't even know him except to see him here."

That made Cameron wonder about his own odd encounter with the man.

"I think I know what the problem is," Summer said.

Cameron raised an eyebrow in question.

"He's lonely," Summer said. "We provide physical sustenance here at Manna. But for many, their time here eating a meal might be the only social interaction they have with other people."

"I think I'm witnessing the birth and development of a new Manna at Common Ground outreach program."

Summer gave him a playful jab. "Maybe not just here at Manna, but across the Common Ground spectrum. Think about it," she said. "Here at Manna we offer food, Bible study, warmth in the winter, air conditioning in the summer, but that's it. The shelter provides a clean bed and a place to shower, but beyond that, it's somewhat isolated, in terms of social interaction."

She was staring over his shoulder and Cameron knew that ideas and scenarios were running through her head: how it could work, what they might need and the like.

"You know what?" Summer said. "I'm going to chat with Mrs. Davidson about this and see what we can legally do."

"Don't you mean with Ilsa Keller?"

She cut her eyes at him.

He held up his hands as if surrendering, then sidestepped that land mine.

"All because you think Sweet Willie is lonely?"

Summer shook her head. "No. Because I think he's probably not the only one of our guests who could use a friend."

Cameron continued serving the remaining Manna guests and praying with two of them, the men who had been arguing over the salt shaker.

While Summer was conjuring up a new outreach

ministry for Common Ground, Cameron was wondering if the city needed to find a way to use the observations of people like Sweet Willie—who were out on the streets all the time—to assist in law enforcement and emergency management.

There was a resource not being tapped. He hoped he'd hear from Willie.

Two days later, Mickey Flynn died of pancreatic cancer at Duke University Medical Center in Durham.

Cameron got the call during the weekly division chiefs' meeting. He bowed his head and remained quiet for several moments. Then he shared the news with his command staff, some of whom had trained under Mickey.

"I'm sorry, Chief," Dave Marsh, his second-in-command, said. "I know the two of you were close."

Cameron let Summer know via a text message, then went to take care of what needed to be done up in Durham.

When he returned to Cedar Springs that night, the silver Mercedes-Benz he knew to be Summer's was parked at the curb in front of his house. Summer was sound asleep in the front seat.

He tapped on the window and she startled awake. "Hey."

She scrambled out of the car and wrapped him in a hug.

"Cam, I'm so sorry about Mickey."

Still numb, Cameron merely nodded. "What are you doing out here?"

Summer reached into the back seat and retrieved a small handled basket. "I made cookies for you," she said, offering him the basket.

Standing in the street, Cameron just stared at it, then he shook his head and hurried up the walkway.

Summer followed. He didn't bar her entry into the house. She set the basket of cookies on the kitchen counter and found Cameron standing in the living room staring at the floor.

"Cam?"

"He had everything done," Cameron said.

Summer came up behind him and put a hand on his shoulder.

Cameron didn't shrug it off, but neither did he lean into the embrace. "Financial bills settled, funeral arrangements made. He saw to it all. All I had to do was sign a few papers. The funeral will be on Wednesday in Raleigh."

"Can I get you something?" Summer asked. "A cup of tea? A cookie?"

Cameron dropped his keys on the coffee table, the sound loud in the stillness.

"Cookies won't make it better, Summer."

The words, harsh, cold and brutal, struck her like a blow.

Tears sprang to her eyes, but she refused to cry. Summer took a deep breath. Grief. This was something she knew a bit about. He was grieving for his friend. It wasn't personal.

Intellectually she understood that he wasn't rejecting her. She'd done what she always did when stressed: she'd baked. Preparing a basket of cookies for Cameron was balm for her, and she'd hoped it would be received as a measure of solace for him, baked and presented in the spirit of love.

"This is the hour of the butterfly."

"What does that mean?"

He shrugged. "Nothing. Just something I heard Mickey say once that made me smile."

Summer settled on the sofa to wait out this phase of mourning with him.

"Summer, it's late. Go home."

She bit her lower lip. "All right, Cam," she said, standing. "I'm truly sorry about Mickey."

When he said nothing at all, Summer, who was no stranger to grief, bit her lip. She hurt for him but also knew that this was a path he had to walk alone. She could be there for him, and would be, but now he needed time to grieve in his own way.

Her mother took the news about Mickey with a calmness that surprised Summer, given the way Lovie had reacted when she heard how sick he was.

"Michael had made his peace with God," Lovie said.

Summer would have asked how she knew that, but the doorbell rang and a couple of her mother's friends from the Women's Club arrived for a committee meeting. After greeting the ladies, Summer slipped out the door to head to a florist shop on Main Street to order flowers for Mickey's service.

Knowing how overwhelming grief and mourning could be, Summer let Cameron know that she was there for him, thinking of him and praying for him. On some level she knew he hadn't meant to rebuff her the way he had. Nevertheless, it stung. And she wondered if in her own grief after her husband's death she, too, had unintentionally hurt the feelings of a friend or neighbor.

This Sunday was supposed to be when Cameron went to service with her at First Memorial. Lovie Darling had talked her daughter into inviting Cameron to join them for Sunday dinner after church and he'd agreed. But that was before...

As Saturday dragged on, Summer eventually gave in and called him. The phone rang straight to voice mail. When she drove out to his house, the driveway where his Lexus was usually parked was empty.

But a few minutes before eleven o'clock Sunday morning, as she entered the doors of First Memorial with her sisters and her mother, she saw him.

Cameron was wearing a dark blue suit and had deep circles under his eyes. He looked emotionally exhausted and Summer's heart went out to him.

He broke into a smile when he saw her, and her

heart did a flip-flop in her chest. She held out her hand and he joined them.

But it was Lovie who stepped forward, taking both of his hands in hers. "I am so sorry for your loss," she told him.

"Thank you," he said.

There wasn't time for more as the service was about to begin.

Cameron sat on the end of the pew on the aisle, with Summer next to him. She studied him as the congregation recited a call to worship.

This wasn't quite how she had envisioned his first visit to her home church.

She wondered if he found First Memorial's worship service stuffy compared to the contemporary and upbeat services of The Fellowship. At First Memorial, they sang songs from the sacred hymn book, exactly three of them. At his church, the words to contemporary Christian songs were beamed on large television screens in the main sanctuary where a six-piece band accompanied the pianist who played an electric keyboard instead of a one-hundred-year-old pipe organ. Tambourines and "amens" rang out in the congregation at The Fellowship, while at First Memorial, the only sound from the congregants might be the occasional cough or a "shh" from the parent of a cranky child.

Mostly, though, as the service progressed, Summer wondered if Cameron needed more time alone. Dinner at her mother's might be too much too soon.

Summer knew he'd taken the death of Mickey Flynn hard—even though he'd known it was coming. A story in Saturday's paper out of Raleigh featured a story on Flynn, who had trained three generations of firefighters.

She squeezed his hand and Cameron looked down at it on the pew.

Dr. Graham's sermon that morning was on forgiveness. It was a subject that Cameron decided had been special-ordered just for him. He felt convicted. Grief was no excuse for rudeness.

He'd been both rude and mean to Summer whose only crime was offering comfort to him. So the last thing he expected or anticipated was being embraced by the Darling women. But they were all treating him as if he might break.

When he'd spotted Summer with her sisters and their mother, it was like watching five beauty pageant contestants walking down the aisle, each one, including their mother, beautiful and striking in her own way. But he had eyes only for Summer.

Mickey was right. Summer was a woman worth fighting for.

Cameron had lost Mickey. And now, due to his own actions, he'd hurt Summer. She was giving him a free pass. He realized that. But there was a window, a window of forgiveness and mercy.

The words to a song sung at The Fellowship came to him: "Great is your mercy."

When the service concluded, Winter and Lovie were properly introduced to him.

"We look forward to seeing you this afternoon," Lovie said.

"Two o'clock," he confirmed.

Lovie nodded. "Come on, girls," she told Spring, Winter and Autumn. "Give them a minute alone."

Summer smiled.

"I'm glad you still came," she said.

"Me, too. Summer, I'm sorry for snapping at you."

She shook her head. "You don't need to apologize for grieving."

She kissed him on the cheek. "See you this afternoon."

Cameron watched her follow her mother and sisters out a side door. When he turned to head toward the entrance he'd used to enter the church, a chapel on the side of the sanctuary caught his eye. He entered the small space, his eyes on a simple crucifix on the front wall.

Unlike the main sanctuary with its stained-glass windows and almost ornate trappings, this space was a place of quiet worship and reflection. Three pews built for no more than six people to sit comfortably were in the chapel, three on each side of the small room. There was no pulpit or lectern in the front—just the spare crucifix on the wall.

Cameron stared at it, then sat in the middle row. He closed his eyes and asked for forgiveness.

"Great *is* your mercy, Lord. I've let my grief and my insecurities get in the way and I've managed in the process to damage the one relationship that means the world to me. Lord, You know my heart. You know I love her even though I haven't had the courage to tell her. Please forgive me, Father. And show me the way to make things right in a way that honors You."

Cameron continued to pray. When he finished, he sat quietly for some time. When he finally opened his eyes and rose to go, he was surprised to see someone else in the chapel.

"Dr. Graham." He stepped forward and offered his hand to the pastor of the First Memorial Church.

"I thought that was you," said the Reverend Doctor Joseph Graham.

He'd removed his vestments and was wearing a dark blue tailored suit with a white shirt and a tie that included flecks of gold and maroon on blue silk. Cameron guessed the suit cost more than everything he himself was wearing. He inwardly winced at the observation. Since he had been seeing Summer Spencer, he had become inordinately preoccupied with how much things cost.

It dawned on him in that moment that he *was* an idiot, just like he'd told Summer.

Of course Summer hadn't invited him to dinner at her mother's home. The one time she'd suggested cooking dinner for him at her house, he'd jumped to the erroneous—as always—conclusion that she was just trying to save him some money.

"Chief Jackson? Are you all right?"

Cameron startled as if surprised to see the minister in front of him. He pumped the man's hand with an unexpected exuberance.

"Yes, Dr. Graham. Yes, I am. Thank you. And thank you for your message today. That was something I needed to hear."

After asking God for forgiveness in the chapel at First Memorial Church, and then realizing that the issues he needed to work on were parallel to what Summer had been going through with the loss of her husband, Cameron left the church with a new-found sense of both peace and purpose.

And he was looking forward to Sunday dinner with the Darling women.

Chapter Sixteen

"Why can't we listen in?" Autumn whined.

"Because we aren't six years old," Spring said. "At least, some of us aren't."

They were in the main kitchen at The Compound, ostensibly putting the finishing touches on a salad for the opening course of the meal, but in reality spying on their sister. Spring lived at the house, but in a wing far removed from her mother's living space. Her own kitchen was not nearly as elaborate as her mother's.

The circular drive at the house looked like a luxury-car-dealer's lot with Summer's Mercedes-Benz, an older model one that had belonged to their father and that Lovie Darling drove occasionally to keep it running. Plus there was a BMW and a Volvo. Cameron's Lexus brought up the rear.

"At least he drives a decent car," Autumn observed.

"When did you get so shallow?" Spring asked.

"When he messed with my sister," Autumn said in full defensive mode.

"Give it a rest, Autumn. You're way too sensitive. The man just lost his best friend and mentor."

"That's still no excuse for making her cry," Autumn said petulantly.

Spring nodded toward the gazebo near the koi pond outside where Summer and Cameron sat. "I think they're working things out."

Autumn brightened. "Really? I liked him before and didn't want him on my permanent nasty list."

"You keep a nasty list?"

Autumn raised an eyebrow. "You'd be surprised."

Spring shook her head. "I don't want to know."

"I'm sorry, Summer," Cameron said. "I had no right to lash out at you the way I did."

They sat next to each other in the gazebo that Lovie Darling had constructed as a respite from the cares of the world. As girls, Summer and her sisters had spent many an afternoon playing dolls on the floor of the structure, and much later, the gazebo was the place for chats and maybe stolen kisses with boyfriends while still under the watchful eyes of either her father or mother, who could and did monitor gazebo activity from the kitchen.

The peaceful oasis was the model Summer had used to develop her own little backyard retreat at the house on Hummingbird Lane. Instead of a gazebo, she had her reflecting bench.

"It's all right, Cam. I understand. We all respond to grief in different ways."

He shook his head. "It's not all right. After you and your family left the church today, I stayed behind for a bit. I found that little chapel off the main sanctuary."

"The prayer chapel," Summer said.

Cameron nodded. "And that's what I did, Summer. I had a revelation," he said.

She glanced over at him waiting for him to voice it.

"I have some issues," he admitted. "Things that it will take me a while to get comfortable with."

"Like the fact that my family is wealthy?"

He nodded. "Yes. That's one. The other is occasionally jumping to conclusions. I've asked the Lord to help me with those things. And I'm asking you to be patient with me as I become a better man."

In the kitchen, Spring nudged Autumn. "See. Told you they'd work it out."

Summer and Cam were holding hands as they walked back to the house.

Autumn grinned. "Do you think we'll eventually get a wedding out of this? I'm ready to be a bridesmaid for one of you."

Spring shook the salad dressing she'd created with oil, vinegar and fresh dried herbs from Lovie's solarium gardening endeavors.

"A few minutes ago, he was on your nasty list.

Now you're ready to witness vows and then throw rice at them?"

Autumn shrugged and snagged a carrot. "If he makes Summer happy, I'm happy."

Spring watched her sister and the fire chief. "It may be a little early to be talking about weddings."

Dinner wasn't the tortured affair that Spring had described, that Summer feared, or that Cameron anticipated.

It began in a cozy parlor with small talk and a salmon mousseline on small, thin slices of a crusty toast. Cameron could have made a meal out of the hors d'oeuvres served by Summer. Luckily, he hadn't been raised by wolves, and despite the desire to reach for the plate, he restricted himself to just two.

"I have something that I'd like to give you, Chief Jackson," Mrs. Darling told him.

Cameron didn't quite know what to make of that.

She went to a side table and returned with a photograph.

"I thought you might like to have this," she said, handing him the small snapshot.

It was of Mickey. He looked to be in his early twenties and was leaning against a fire truck. "Mrs. Darling, I can't take your photo."

She patted his hand. "Michael always knew what he wanted to do," she said. "I sense you probably have a lot of Michael in you, too. This is something you should have."

Cameron stared at the image of his mentor, then met Lovie Darling's gaze. "Thank you."

She nodded, and with that, Mrs. Darling, dressed in the yellow chiffon-enhanced suit she'd worn to church, guided them all in to dinner.

They ate in a formal dining room on a table of dark wood and on china that complemented an exquisite table setting. If he hadn't actually been seated at the table Cameron would have thought he was looking at a photo shoot from one of the home decorating magazines his mother loved to read. Had he been in anyone else's home, he would have asked to take a picture of the table with his smartphone to email to his mother. *That* wasn't going to happen here. He'd have to remember the details to share with her.

Fresh cut flowers in pale creams, pinks and delicate blues formed a centerpiece that did not impede conversation or vision. The dinner plates carried the same color scheme and had a delicate scalloped edging trimmed in gold. Cam noticed that the flatware had the heft and sheen of real silver, not the stainless steel that his own knives, forks and spoons were made of. And the goblets were cut crystal.

Despite the luxury, the table's occupants, including Cameron, were at ease. The dinner didn't seem formal, but comfortable, the way a family's Sunday meal was supposed to be.

The Darling women were gracious Southern hostesses.

Mrs. Darling sat at the head of the table and Cameron was opposite her. He guessed that the sisters, Summer to his right with Spring next to her, and Autumn and Winter on the opposite side, sat in the places where they'd been sitting down to supper all of their lives.

He noticed that his chair had arms and the others didn't. He wondered if, for some reason, he had been placed at the head of the table.

The salad of fresh greens included arugula, spinach, diced apricot, shaved carrots and some other green Cameron didn't recognize. It was followed by a stuffed filet of sole that had Cameron wondering how soon he could wrangle another invitation to dinner at the Darling residence.

He lifted his water goblet to Mrs. Darling and complimented her on the dish.

"My contribution to the meal was minimal," Mrs. Darling said. "The girls take turns on the second Sunday."

"Except for Winter," Autumn said. "You *really* don't want her cooking for you."

"If what she does is considered cooking," Summer said with a wink at Winter.

"A microwave is a perfectly acceptable cooking device," Winter said in her own defense.

Laughter greeted that pronouncement.

Cameron enjoyed the byplay and teasing among the sisters.

"I have to confess," Spring said. "You all were my guinea pigs today with the sole. I debated about what to stuff it with—crabmeat or shrimp. I was trying out a recipe for the supper club."

Winter and Autumn groaned.

"What?" Cameron asked.

"The Magnolia Supper Club is our dear Spring's little monthly soirée," Summer said for his benefit.

"One to which none of us has ever been invited," Winter groused.

"You have to cook to be invited," Spring said, and apparently not for the first time because Autumn mimicked the words even as the eldest Darling sister spoke them.

Cameron grinned.

"And," Spring said, "for your information, Miss Microwave Chef of the year, Summer has been invited."

Winter rolled her eyes.

"I haven't decided yet if I want to participate," Summer said. "I like to experiment with baking, not all of the other things like entrées and appetizers."

Lovie Darling chuckled. "Chief Jackson, don't let this bickering fool you. Spring's supper club is a recurring bone of contention among those two," she said with a nod toward Spring and Winter. "The members of the Magnolia Supper Club have very discerning palates."

"That's Mother's kind way of saying they are all hoity-toity foodies," Winter said, "who would never let a frozen chicken nugget or a deep-fried Twinkie pass their lips. Only foie gras, truffles and arugula for that bunch. They all think they should be hosting their own programs on one of those cooking channels."

"There was arugula in your salad and I didn't hear any complaints as you scarfed it down a few minutes ago," Spring said.

Summer made a face. "Deep-fried Twinkies?"

Autumn shook her head. "Here we go." To Cameron she said, "Consider yourself initiated, Chief Cam. Every time it's either Winter's or Spring's turn to cook for a Second Sunday we have this debate. It's like listening to a scratched CD. Irritating."

"Can we please change the subject?" Spring asked.

"I agree," Lovie said, much in the manner of the head of a judicial body issuing a final decree.

"Have arrangements been made for Michael?" Lovie asked Cameron, steering the conversation in an entirely different direction.

"Yes. He had everything done ahead of time."

Lovie nodded. "Michael was like that. Always prepared, always thinking ahead."

She seemed lost in thought for a long moment. Summer and her siblings studied their mother, but no one said anything. Eventually Lovie expelled a breath that seemed to be equal parts wistfulness, regret and grief. She closed her eyes for a second, and then expressed her delight about the choir's choice of selections for the morning service.

"It's nice to see them add something new to the choral repertoire."

The conversation then flowed as if the six of them regularly sat down to a shared Sunday meal. They talked about the weather, movies and a novel that they'd all read in the last six months.

"With the fire department keeping you so busy," Lovie Darling said, "I'm surprised you have time to read fiction, Chief."

The air seemed to be sucked out of the dining room as four pairs of blue eyes turned to Lovie and the sisters held their collective breaths.

Here we go, he thought.

Mickey notwithstanding, the pleasantries were over and she clearly wanted to know about the peasant dating her daughter. But Cameron had to chuckle to himself. He'd specifically asked the Lord to teach him to work through just this sort of situation. Mrs. Darling's comment could have easily provoked him into believing it was intended as a slight to a working man. But today, Cameron had learned a lesson or two. The first lesson was that being slow to anger or take offense was a virtue he wanted to cultivate. And second, that there was usually more than one way to handle a potentially awkward situation.

He gave Mrs. Darling a self-deprecating smile. "That's why it took me about three months to finish reading it," he said. "I usually catch up on my reading when I go on vacation. With uninterrupted time to read and relax, I go through about half a dozen novels. Have you read the new mystery by Henrietta Wright Worthy?"

The mention of Cedar Springs' celebrated mystery writer eased the tension and launched them all into a spirited debate over the author's narrative arc in her novels.

Summer beamed at him, and Cameron smiled back.

The dinner was a success.

"Who's going to help me with dessert?" Spring asked.

"I will," Summer said.

"And I'll get the coffee," Autumn said. "Come help, Winter."

"But…"

Autumn tugged on her sister's blouse and Winter got up, mumbling about supper club rejects.

"They aren't very subtle, are they, Chief Jackson?" Lovie said from her seat opposite his.

He smiled. "I was wondering if it was something I said."

"When the girls were younger, if one of them brought a young man home for dinner, they made themselves scarce so their father could interrogate the poor boy."

Cameron held his tongue. He knew from Summer and from her older sister that if any interrogating of young men had been done, it was Lovie Darling leading the inquisition.

"I want to thank you for two things, Chief Jackson."

"Yes, ma'am?"

"First, for joining us for Sunday dinner. It's nice to see a man in that chair again."

Cameron's guess had been right. He *had* been seated in Dr. John Darling's place at the dining table.

"And most of all," Lovie said, "I want to thank you for making my daughter happy."

The compliment took him by surprise, but even more surprising was the moisture he thought he saw in Lovie Darling's eyes. A moment later, it was confirmed when she delicately dabbed a corner of her linen napkin at the corner of an eye.

"Summer has had a difficult time," she said. "I'm glad she's found happiness again, and that joy has taken over the sadness in her eyes. You put that joy there, Chief Jackson. Thank you."

Cameron found himself a bit choked up, too.

He didn't quite know what to say. Lovie Darling wasn't the dread force of nature he had been expecting to encounter. She was a woman who clearly loved her daughters and wanted to see them happy.

And she was a woman who had made a difficult decision decades ago. She chose to follow her heart. In doing so, she'd broken the heart of his friend.

But Cameron was glad that Mickey and Lovie Darling had been able to have a few moments together before Mickey's death. He'd been stunned, but pleasantly surprised when the nurses told him about Mickey's visitor who was clearly not someone from the fire service.

"Mrs. Darling," he said.

She lifted an eyebrow in answer, a gesture that he recognized from Summer. "Yes, Chief Jackson?"

"Please," he said. "Call me Cameron."

Chapter Seventeen

The funeral service for Mickey Flynn was truly a firefighters' send-off. Hundreds of people, neighbors, church members, friends, city officials and a seemingly never-ending line of firefighters all in uniform, showed up to say farewell.

"I have some duties to perform," Cameron told Summer, "so we won't be able to sit together."

"I know," Summer told him as she slipped her hand in his. Cameron, in the formal dress blue uniform and spit-shined shoes that he'd worn when he showed up at her front door, was somber, but not stoic. His grieving was, Summer suspected, a private affair. "My mother is here," she said. "We'll sit together."

An honor guard, also in formal dress blues, had the colors posted at the church. Mickey's family consisted of his fire department brethren and Cameron.

The service was both in honor of and respect for

a man who was responsible for nurturing the careers of so many men and women. Just about every one of them spoke highly of him, including more than a dozen former students who, like Cameron, were now fire chiefs in their own right. There were proclamations from elected officials, and then there was a tribute to his faith in song.

As former student after former student spoke about him, Summer realized just how much he'd meant to not only Cameron, but all of the men and women he'd mentored through the years. At one point, Lovie reached for Summer's hand and squeezed it tight.

When Cameron rose to go to the podium he walked straight and tall. He was 100 percent male and for the first time in her life Summer realized the appeal a man in uniform had to many women.

She'd dated a Marine from Camp Lejeune while in college. That short-lived relationship had been based on sheer curiosity on both of their parts. But there were plenty of girls she'd attended high school and college with who looked no further than Fort Bragg and the Marine Corps base to find their life partners.

A uniform didn't make the man, Summer thought as Cameron pulled a few index cards from a pocket. But it sure made the man look good.

She hadn't known that he'd prepared remarks.

"I put together a few things to say about Mickey,"

he began holding up the cards to the gathered mourners. "But a lot of what I have written here has been said today already. So I would like to spend a few moments telling you about the Mickey Flynn I knew."

Cameron cleared his throat and Summer's heart gave a little flip. Sitting in the church at Mickey Flynn's funeral she realized she had fallen in love with this man. Despite her best efforts, she'd done the one thing she thought she would never do again—fall head over heels, heart and soul in love with someone.

With a tissue in hand, she listened to him bare his soul about his friend.

He touched his hand to his brow for a moment and gave a half smile. "Just recently, I had the occasion to explain to someone dear to me why I do what I do."

Cameron's gaze found Summer's in the crowd. She could not keep the astonishment from her face. A wry smile tugged at Cameron's mouth, and Summer felt heat flame her cheeks at the personal reference. She managed—just barely—to squelch the involuntary sound of surprise in the hushed sanctuary.

"That desire to work in fire service comes from a place deep down," Cameron said, tapping his chest for emphasis. "It is an opportunity to serve others, to save lives, to learn and to live discipline, teamwork and to be a part of something bigger than a single person. For Mickey, it was even more than that.

"Mickey loved firefighting and he loved God," Cameron said. "For some people, finding the connection between faith and fire service might seem something of a stretch. But Mickey gave all of us the model and the example of why and how to experience joy, pure joy, in helping other people and in showing compassion for others. With a servant's heart he was able to do his job as a sacrifice to God."

Summer dabbed at her eyes and saw that her mother was doing the same thing.

Listening to Cameron talk about his friend, she understood even more about him. Cameron was a man who displayed faith in his actions, and so, apparently, had been Mickey Flynn.

"I was honored to claim Michael Sean Flynn as a mentor and friend," Cameron said. "I was proud to serve with him as a fellow firefighter, and today, though we mourn the passing of the man, I am filled with joy because I know that Mickey is in glory, sitting on the right hand of the Father and looking down at all of us left here to carry on his work."

When Cameron took his seat again in front with the other fire chiefs, Summer swallowed the lump in her throat.

She understood.

She understood his initial reaction when she tried

to express her own sadness at his loss. Cookies did not make it better. But she was glad that Cameron had had those days at the end to spend time with Mickey. And a glance at her mother revealed another truth: Lovie was crying, but she looked content. Her mother had made the right choice all those years ago.

A poem about firefighting was recited. Then the final tolling of the fire bell brought her and everyone else gathered to tears. During the drive to the cemetery in a processional that began with the No. 1 truck from Mickey's station and his flag-draped coffin on a caisson and lasted for blocks of cars and fire trucks, Cameron held Summer's hand as they drove, mostly in silence.

After the funeral and graveside services, there was a repast at the fire station closest to Mickey's home. By six o'clock that evening, Cameron and Summer were headed back to Cedar Springs from Raleigh.

"There had to have been a thousand people there," Summer said later.

Cameron nodded. "That's why the service was at that church instead of St. Paul's, which is Mickey's church, but has a small sanctuary."

"Thank you for letting me share this day with you," she told Cameron.

Cameron squeezed her hand then returned both to the wheel. "I'm glad you were there."

"That poem," she said, reaching for her handbag where she had tucked the funeral program. "It echoed what you've been telling me."

Cameron nodded. "It's recited at most firefighters' funerals. It began as an actual prayer of a Wichita fireman after a call-out to an apartment fire where kids were trapped. What's printed in the program there is the way it's been altered over the years. There are other versions," he said with a glance at Summer, "including one called 'A Fireman's Wife's Prayer.'"

"Really?"

He nodded again. "But all across the country, 'The Fireman's Prayer' is inscribed on monuments to firefighters killed in the line of duty. Mickey's funeral was a little different in that regard."

"What do you mean?"

"He died of cancer, but was honored with the funeral rites of a line-of-duty death."

Summer nodded. "Well, I'm glad I got to know more about Mickey through you and all of his protégés today. A lot of people lost…" she paused and reached for Cameron's hand. "*You* lost a good friend and mentor. I'm sorry."

He was quiet for so long that Summer grew concerned. "Cam?"

"Mickey was assured in his faith," he said. "But you know what I'm most grateful for, in addition to his friendship?"

She smiled. "What's that?"

"That he and your mom had a chance to reconnect before he died."

Chapter Eighteen

Several days later, Summer knocked on the door of the small office that Ilsa Keller used on the days when she came to Manna. Her stomach had been in knots from the moment she'd awakened. She found herself equal parts relieved and dismayed that the day had finally arrived for the two of them to talk.

For the briefest of moments, before Ilsa put on one of her fake smiles, Summer glimpsed raw animosity on her face.

Summer took a step back.

"Come in, Summer. You're right on time."

Summer was ten minutes early, but she didn't correct her.

"Have a seat," Ilsa invited, indicating one of two uncomfortable-looking chairs in front of the desk.

The space was tight, the room barely large enough for a desk, the two chairs and a four-drawer file cabinet. An older-model desktop computer took up most of the space on the desk.

Both Cameron and Spring thought quitting her volunteer work at Manna was a bad idea. As of six o'clock this morning, Summer had remained conflicted.

Ilsa, dressed in blue slacks and a cream blouse, settled behind the desk and clasped her hands together on the blotter.

"You wanted to meet with me?"

Summer nodded, pulling her thoughts together.

"When I moved to Cedar Springs," she began, "I wanted to get immersed in the community. I heard about Manna at Common Ground in church one Sunday and thought it might be the perfect vehicle for merging my interests and skills."

She took a deep breath. So far, so good, but she couldn't sugarcoat what came next. "I've enjoyed the work here tremendously. Manna offers a tremendous service to people in need."

"But you're quitting," Ilsa said.

Summer was startled by both the resignation in Ilsa's voice and the fact that she'd surmised the reason for the meeting request.

"I…"

Ilsa held up a hand to halt her next words.

"It's my fault," Ilsa said. "Manna has been losing volunteers left and right for the last six months. Long before you got here. I didn't like you on sight."

Summer jerked. She couldn't have been more surprised by the verbal attack.

"What? Why?"

A rueful smile flashed across Ilsa's mouth and was gone as quickly as it had come. "I thought you were my replacement."

"Your replacement? But I'd just moved back here. I don't have any experience running a soup kitchen. I just wanted something to do a few days of the week."

Ilsa snorted. "So you say."

"Ilsa, I asked to meet with you because I wanted to make some suggestions about how to more effectively schedule volunteers. Manna needs a volunteer coordinator so all of the work can be done without burdening any one or two people."

"Everything was running smoothly," Ilsa said.

"Then why were volunteers quitting left and right?"

The question was out of Summer's mouth before she could squelch it.

Ilsa smiled, but it held no humor or warmth. "Well," she said, pushing her chair back from the desk and bending down. "That's not my problem anymore."

"What do you mean?"

The soup kitchen director hefted a small box up from the floor. A handbag was on top of it.

"I've been relieved of my duties here," she said. "The Common Ground board so very graciously offered to keep me for another month while they searched for a new director. I told them I'd be leaving immediately."

Summer stood. "Ilsa, I don't understand."

"Yes, you do, Summer. Congratulations on the new job."

While Summer was meeting with Ilsa Keller, Cameron was driving across town to Elmhurst Street. The call he'd gotten summoning him to the scene of a house fire had him thinking about Sweet Willie, the homeless man from the soup kitchen.

Willie knew something was going on on Elmhurst Street, and now there was a fire on the street. The call-out wasn't to the house that the police chief was concerned about, but the coincidence didn't sit well with Cameron.

He pulled the department SUV in behind the second fire truck at the scene and assessed the situation. An ambulance sat idling and a police cruiser was also in the street, its siren off but lights flashing.

The blaze was under control and one crew was already packing up. The crew captain jogged across the lawn and over to him.

"Hello, Chief."

"What's the sitrep?"

The fire captain filled in the details: a neighbor spotted flames from the shed, had his wife call 911 while he ran over with a garden hose.

"That actually put out the fire."

Cameron frowned. "So why am I here, Charlie?"

The fire captain jerked his head. "This way,

Chief. It's what—or rather who—the neighbor found out back."

"What do you mean who?"

"In the backyard was our suspect, Peter Bradley."

Cameron followed the captain around the house, noting the For Sale sign as they passed by. The backyard of the two-story house was cordoned off with crime-scene tape.

"Young Mr. Bradley, that would be the seventeen-year-old, was out cold. Apparently, after starting the fire he went dashing across the yard and ran into a rake. Stepped on it and it conked him in the head."

Cameron chuckled.

"I know," Charlie said. "It's not funny, but it is. He has a big knot on his forehead but he'll live. He's mad at his brother and is ratting him out. So far, he's copped to at least three of our unsolved fires. Peter says his brother put the rake there deliberately to trip him."

"Stupid criminals," Cameron said.

"Yep," Charlie said.

"Unfortunately, this one is a juvie. Parents?"

"The mother's on her way up from Bragg. Single mom, works at the base. The boys have a lot of unsupervised time on their hands."

"And the older brother? Where is he?" Cameron asked his captain.

"Home, according to Bradley the younger. A couple of units are there now. Haven't heard back on his status."

Cameron clapped Charlie on the back. "Nice work. Thanks."

While the captain went to oversee the final cleanup at the house, Cameron made his way back to the truck. This scene fit the pattern of the other fires. The house on Elmhurst was empty so presumably no one would be injured if the backyard shed went up in smoke. A preliminary assessment had it looking like they'd gotten to the bottom of the recent fires.

The Bradley brothers were a couple of budding pyromaniacs. Maybe with some counseling the tendency would get nipped before they escalated to bigger blazes and hurt or killed someone.

At Manna, Summer stood in the kitchen trying to get a handle on what had just happened with Ilsa. Mrs. Davidson typically knew everything that went on at Common Ground, but her office was empty.

If the director had just walked out the door, who was going to run the place?

A check of the volunteer schedule showed that there were enough people to cover the day—if they all showed up.

Summer was torn. Should she leave and go get her errands done or stay and help out in case an extra pair of hands was needed?

The question was answered when the door opened and three volunteers bustled in.

"Hi, Summer!" Jocelyn Reynolds said. "I didn't know you were working today."

Summer greeted the ladies, then put the strap of her purse over her shoulder. "I'm not. I just stopped by. It looks like you're fully staffed. So I'm on my way out."

The knots that had caused the uneasiness in her stomach were gone. As she waved farewell to Jocelyn and the others, she knew that she'd been drawn home to Cedar Springs to start over.

Maybe if there really was an opening for a director for Manna at Common Ground, she had what it would take to fill the position.

Chapter Nineteen

For Summer, the next day was one to be endured. That was all that she could hope for. Today, she slipped off the gold chain that her wedding and engagement rings from Garrett hung from. She put them on her ring finger. She stared at her hand for a long, long time before returning the rings and the chain to her jewelry box.

She'd heard from Cameron, but only via a short text saying he had to work and wouldn't be able to see her. Summer took that as a sign from the Lord that she needed some space to breathe, today of all days—the second anniversary of the day Garrett died.

But the message she got from on high at noon knocked her for an emotional loop she should have seen coming, but somehow hadn't.

She made a light lunch, half of a vegetarian cheese melt and a cup of the tea specially blended for her by the proprietor of Tea Time on Main

Street. She had no appetite though, and only nibbled on the sandwich, barely eating two complete bites. She gave up, and took her tea into the sunroom. She clicked on the flat-screen television mounted on the wall as she headed to one of the chaises. The midday news had already started, and from the sound of things, it was all bad news.

She put the mug on the floor and gripped the remote control as she registered just what she was seeing on the television screen above a Breaking News banner with the location: Cedar Springs.

A nearly breathless newscaster reported from the scene of a huge fire. Summer fumbled with the remote, pushing up the volume.

"At this hour, we know that two firefighters have been transported," the TV reporter said. "The extent of their injuries has not yet been confirmed. It has taken some time for the crews to get this blaze under control."

Summer watched slack-jawed as the television station ran footage of firefighters dragging a fallen colleague from a warehouse that looked more like something conjured out of Hollywood than a real fire. But the Cedar Springs Fire Department logo on the fire trucks belied that.

As the television live spot continued, Summer scrambled for her cell phone.

A part of her knew it was unreasonable, but she called Cameron's number. It rang to voice mail.

She sent a text, but didn't expect a reply.

Shaking with fear, she dashed back to the television.

"...that's all we know at this hour. This is Sasha Calloway, reporting to you live from the scene of this three-alarm fire in Cedar Springs. Back to you, Annette."

The flames burned hot and wild on the television.

Summer let out a whimper, the news far more than she could bear.

Summer tried Cameron's number again, even knowing as she did so that it was unreasonable to expect him to answer. He was fire chief, a chief who went out on calls and this was a big one. A really big one.

"Calm down, Summer," she said aloud in an attempt to coach herself through the panic. "He's okay. He's okay."

Then a thought struck her. He might *not* be okay. Cameron could be one of the injured. And even if he wasn't, some of the firefighters she'd met and knew might be the ones who were hurt.

"Oh, Lord. Please protect them all."

The entreaty served as a balm. Instantly, Summer knew that wringing her hands and going out of her mind with fear was not what she needed to be doing right now. She'd done that two years ago and it had changed not one thing. She thought of Mickey Flynn and the poem printed on his funeral program.

She went to the foyer basket where she'd placed the program. At the funeral, "The Firefighter's Prayer" had been recited by two fire chief friends of Mickey's. She'd gotten a chill that day as they read the verses. Now she understood why it had moved her so much. And she finally understood what Cameron had been trying to tell her for so long.

"I want to fill my calling
To give the best in me,
To guard my friend and neighbor
And protect their property."

Firefighting was dangerous work. The many verses of the poem attributed to Alvin William Linn confirmed for Summer what Cameron was all about.

Fire service was a calling that most people eschewed. But one that, for Cameron and Mickey Flynn, defined who and what they were: men of faith and honor.

She clung to that as she pushed open the sliding glass doors that led to her deck and backyard. Crossing the lawn, she made her way to a tranquil oasis: a flower bed planted in a semicircle with a white cast-iron bench with cozy padded cushions placed nearby for quiet contemplation. Instead of sitting on what she'd deemed her reflecting bench, Summer got to her knees and braced her elbows on the cushioned seat.

Clasping her hands together, she bowed her head and closed her eyes.

"Father God, You know what today is and You know my state of mind," she began.

Summer always prayed as if she were talking to God, having a one-on-one conversation with a dear and precious friend. The words of her prayer flowed from a place deep within her, a place where her faith began and flowered.

"Please, please, please keep him safe. I know it's not about my will, but Yours that matters. I just don't know if I could survive all of that again.

"Lord, I'm not being a drama queen, really, I'm not. I just... Lord, please keep Cameron safe. Provide Your healing touch to those who have been injured.

"I pray for the families of those firefighters who must be anxious right now. Lord, please give them...and me...a measure of peace and comfort at this hour. I pray and lift up Jose and Billy and Malik and Chip and Rob. Those are the names I remember, but You know all of them, Lord. And I ask that you blanket each one with Your grace, Your mercy, Your protection and Your love. Amen."

Then Summer rose. She sat on the bench and contemplated the beauty and the miracle of the flowers in her garden.

But she couldn't stop her hands from trembling.

It was well after seven that night when he found her at the Darling family's historic farmhouse. After giving him the directions to the property, Spring suggested he try the front-porch swing first. If he didn't see Summer there, he would need to go to the old silo. While other kids had tree houses that they climbed into and played in, the Darling sisters had a silo at what had been their grandparents' farm.

When he saw the porch swing empty, Cameron sighed. He parked his car and headed toward the silo. The structure was just as Spring described it and there at the top, sitting precariously on the edge, was Summer.

He didn't dare holler up. He didn't want to startle her.

So despite his reservations and concern, Cameron followed the directions he'd been given on how to get into and up the old structure. She had to have heard him, but she didn't say anything.

He then joined Summer, his feet dangling into nothingness. He figured climbing up here was the least he could do given the circumstances.

"Summer? Can you tell me what we're doing up here?"

The question, voiced in as calm a manner as he could manage, seemed reasonable to Cameron. But reason didn't seem to be on today's menu. As Cedar Springs' fire chief, he was used to being in dangerous places. Today's fire was one example. This, however, seemed like unnecessary danger, and bordered on ridiculous.

"Summer, honey, I need you to talk to me."

The pretty blonde sitting next to him had become more than a town resident who needed the assistance of the fire department to check out the smoke alarms in her new home. She'd managed to worm her way into his heart, a heart he thought immune to country club beauties and trust fund babies—people who knew little or nothing about making an honest day's living.

Summer had proved him wrong on both counts, even though she was both a trust fund daughter and appeared more suited to the country club than the sometimes mean streets of Cedar Springs.

And yet he'd found himself head over heels in love with her. He wanted her to be his wife—even if he didn't deserve her. Her wanted her to stand by him for the rest of his days.

But before he could voice any of that, they needed to get down off this fifty-foot silo.

She leaned forward, looking down.

Cameron's heart stopped.

Was she suicidal?

It didn't seem like it, but she was calm. Too calm.

He reached for her arm and clasped it, not too fast or too strong, but with a sure grip. He didn't want to scare her. She was already doing a great job of scaring the daylights out of him.

"I'm not going to jump, Cameron." Her voice, barely above a whisper and sounding a lot to Cameron like she didn't mean what she said.

"Then why don't we get down from here," he

said, the voice of smooth and non-threatening reason. "I know we had a fight. I'm sorry. Really."

Given that they were perched on the edge of a pitched roof silo adjacent to a building that looked like it needed to be demolished rather than restored, smooth and non-threatening was definitely the order of the day.

She glanced over at him and Cameron saw a sadness in her eyes that he'd never seen before.

"It's not dangerous," she said. "When we were kids, we used to come up here all the time. It was like a hideaway for me and my sisters."

"Hmm."

She smiled, but it didn't reach her eyes. "I've learned to interpret that particular sound of skepticism. I'm not going to jump, Cameron," she said again. "I came up here to think. It's a soothing place for me."

He still held her arm.

"Can we maybe do some thinking on terra firma?"

"You can see almost to Fayetteville from up here," Summer said, ignoring his request. "At least that's what I always used to think when I was a girl. When I got mad at my sisters or at Daddy, I used to come up here, stare out at the horizon and declare that just as soon as I could, I was going to escape from Cedar Springs, move to Fayetteville and marry a soldier or maybe go down to Camp Lejeune, where I'd meet and fall in love with a marine."

She shrugged his arm away and pulled her legs

up over the edge of the silo. She was barefoot, Cameron noticed. She must have left her shoes at the bottom of that seemingly never-ending and rickety ladder he'd climbed to get up here.

Sitting with her knees bent and her hands wrapped around them, she glanced at him and then away.

"Something about a man in uniform?" he asked, hoping his voice held the levity he strived for.

When she smiled this time, the waning sun seemed to shine a little brighter in the summer sky. Her eyes sparkled and a bit of color reddened her cheeks.

"Apparently I never got over that uniform thing. I'm falling in love with another man in a uniform."

As far as Cameron knew, her husband hadn't been military, not active, retired or reserve corps. Bitter disappointment shrouded his soul. He swallowed back the bile that rose at the thought of Summer with another man. Is this what Mickey felt when the love of his life had left him for someone else?

Cameron was a grown-up. He'd dealt with rejection before and would do so again.

As he'd overheard her mother talking at the City Council meeting—a meeting that with everything that had happened since seemed like months ago—he wasn't the right kind of man for a Darling woman. He was the rebound man, the get-back-into-the-swing-of-things man, before she found another cardiologist or surgeon to settle down with.

Maybe it wouldn't hurt so much since she had no way of knowing how he really felt about her.

Yeah, right.

"So," he started, trying and probably failing, but not caring at this point. "Who is the lucky man?"

He wanted to know so maybe he could go punch his lights out. A part of Cameron knew that thought wasn't very Christian. But the part of him whose heart was breaking over losing Summer to another man didn't care.

"It's you," she said. "But I doubt if you'd call that lucky."

Cameron blinked, and shook his head as if to clear it after suffering a blow. If he had not already been holding on practically for dear life, he would likely have tumbled right over the edge of the silo.

His heart suddenly beat a staccato.

Cameron felt like he had been waiting his entire life to hear this woman declare that she loved him as much as he loved her. But right now, he was pretty sure that he was dreaming.

"Excuse me?"

She looked at him. None of the light he'd come to associate with her was there. Summer looked miserable.

"You heard me," she said, the confirmation barely a mumble.

If he could pinpoint the exact moment when he

fell hard for her, it was the moment she had fallen into his arms at her front door even though he'd fought it every step of the way since then. It was not just the physical attraction or the protectiveness he felt toward her, it was the knowledge that came from deep within that this was the woman he was meant to be with.

But he needed to be sure.

"You love me?"

"Against my better judgment," Summer said, her tone morose.

"Generally, when someone tells someone else that they love them, it is perceived as a good thing. But that's not really the vibe I'm getting right now."

The corners of her mouth lifted up for a millisecond, but the movement could in no way be defined as a full-fledged smile.

Summer wrapped her arms around her waist and leaned forward.

There was no danger of her falling over the edge from where she sat now, but Cameron automatically reached out to steady her.

"Cam, I'm fine. Really," she said. "Well, that's not really true. Part of me is fine. The other part, the part that has fallen in love with you, is terrified. And I don't like being afraid. It's debilitating. It feels…" She shrugged. "It's scary."

"As scary as sitting up on this silo?"

That earned him an honest smile.

He scooted over and tugged on one of her hands

until he captured it in his. He threaded his fingers with hers.

"Talk to me, Summer. Don't shut me out. Please."

She swallowed, then took a deep breath. "Loving you is dangerous," she said.

He waited.

"Loving you is dangerous because what you do is dangerous," Summer said. "And that, well, that's on me. It's something that I'll have to figure out how to deal with."

Summer sighed and Cameron held his breath, afraid that she was about to take away the gift of her love just moments after declaring it.

"There's something you need to know," Summer said. "Something about me that's important."

"Okay," Cameron said.

Summer gazed into his eyes.

"Even though you're the chief, you are first and foremost a firefighter," she said. "When we first met, well, when we *first* met, I, of course, was just coming to. But you intrigued me even then."

"And that was a bad thing?"

She smiled. "No, it was a… It was disconcerting. After Garrett died, a part of me died, too. The ability to feel. When I met you, there was feeling again and it scared me." She held up a hand to ward off any interjection he might make. "Not because of the circumstances, but because a part of me felt like I was being unfaithful to Garrett in even being

attracted to another man. And to add insult to in-
jury, that that other man was you—a firefighter—
was worse."

A surge of jealousy tried to rear its head. But
Cameron wanted so desperately for this to work
with this woman who had captured his heart and
soul. He needed to make sure he was not missing
or overlooking any important detail. That she was
obviously in turmoil ate at him.

"So there's some bad history with you and a firefighter?"

Summer shook her head. "No. But I—I'm getting to that."

He took her hands in his, silently encouraging
her to go on while also conveying that he was there
with her on the arduous journey of baring her soul
to him.

"In order to make it all right, I told myself—I
convinced myself—that a fire chief wasn't so bad."

She winced and he realized that he had uncon-
sciously tightened his grip.

There it was again. It was always about class and
economics with her.

Summer Darling Spencer was, after all, a daughter, a granddaughter and a widow of wealth.

As the Cedar Springs fire chief, Cameron made
an honest living at a comfortable salary. He was far
from rich, but he was doing okay. And, apparently,
okay did not make the cut with the country club set.

"Firefighting is dangerous, but it is honest and honorable work," he said.

"What?" Summer blinked, confusion etched on her face.

"Everybody can't be a wealthy doctor like your father and your husband, Summer. I had hoped that you were…"

"Stop! There you go again! That's not what I'm saying at all."

She snatched her hands away from him, then scooted back, farther away from him where she sat cross-legged, the distance between them suddenly more than physical.

"I'm not articulating this very well," she said.

He ran his hand through his hair in a frustrated gesture. "Then help me understand, Summer."

"Yes, Garrett was a cardiologist, and we were well-off, very well-off. But money wasn't the issue. It was the danger. He constantly put himself in harm's way, and that's what killed him."

"I don't understand. What danger?"

Suddenly the words were tumbling from her mouth in a torrent of fear and angst. Tears cascaded down her cheeks and she swiped them away.

"I'm afraid," she said. "I'm afraid that if I let myself love you wholeheartedly, unconditionally and unabashedly the way my heart tells me to, that you'll die, too. You will die in some horribly fiery way just like Garrett did and I don't think I can take that kind of heartbreak again. I can't do it," she said again. "It hurts too much."

Cameron's heart slammed into his chest.

Die in some horribly fiery way just like Garrett.

He realized then that he had made a mistake… a terrible, terrible mistake. He'd let his insecurities about the differences in their economic stations cloud both his judgment and his ability to understand that Summer's anxiety and hesitancy had nothing to do with his social class or bank account balance. He had completely misread her and the situation.

With his thumb, he wiped away the tears that fell from her eyes. Cameron reached for her hands, tugging them from around her knees and pulled her into his embrace.

"Summer, honey, it's okay. I'm here."

Cameron had badly misjudged her, letting his own insecurities overshadow the truth his heart had known from the moment he met this special woman.

On the top of the silo at her family's old farm, he rocked her until the tears subsided. Then, lowering his head, he pressed his lips to hers, the kiss one of healing and apology, of love and his silent plea for her forgiveness.

For a long quiet moment they just sat on the silo, each drawing comfort and strength from the other as the sun began to set and dusk fell across the

North Carolina sky. But her words still echoed in Cameron's head.

"Summer, tell me what happened to Garrett."

Chapter Twenty

Summer wiped at her eyes and scolded herself for being such an emotional wreck.

She hated that there was so much unspent emotion bottled up inside of her. When Garrett died she thought she had cried enough tears to last at least a dozen years. But here she was, crying all over Cameron like she didn't know how to turn off the waterworks.

"Garrett died in a car wreck," she said, finally answering his request to know what happened.

Cameron stroked her arm, providing solace but not interrupting. Summer was grateful for the space.

"Yes, he was a doctor, like Daddy. But unlike my father, who spent his free time doing church work or taking us out on weekend getaways, Garrett liked danger. Saving lives didn't give him the satisfaction that he craved. To this day I think that had he been a trauma surgeon in an emergency room, the thrill he needed, the adrenaline that got him pumped up, would have been fulfilled, especially if he worked in a large metropolitan hospital in a city like Atlanta or Charlotte. But Garrett was a specialist, and a top-tier specialist at that."

She glanced up at Cameron to see how her words were being received. He simply waited. He offered no commentary. He simply waited for her to tell the story in her own time and way.

Summer sighed.

"Don't get me wrong," she said. "He worked hard, really hard. And he liked to play as hard as he worked. We didn't have kids so the time and money he put into his little hobby wasn't an issue. It was the danger that concerned me. But Garrett always laughed it off."

She cast her blue eyes at him in one last, maybe desperate plea to just leave the past where it lay. But Summer knew she owed Cameron this explanation. He deserved to know the root of her anxieties, the reason she remained single despite both her mother's efforts and the efforts of many gentlemen who admired both her beauty and her bank accounts. And the reason behind her collapse at her front door the day they'd met.

"Garrett raced cars in his free time," she finally said. "And I don't mean drag racing in a parking lot. He raced, as in stock car racing, NASCAR level. Two hundred miles an hour on professional courses. He was good, good enough to have actually qualified had medicine not been his first gig. He talked about giving up his practice to race. He even sponsored a couple of NASCAR drivers before eventually buying some shares in one of the teams."

"What happened?" Cameron asked softly.

"Garrett had a recklessness in him. It was something we argued about on the few occasions when we actually had fights. I think it was born of the fact that he didn't get to choose his destiny. Before he was born, his parents knew he would be a doctor just like they were and his grandparents before him. Race car driving was his secret passion."

She fell silent again, thinking about Garrett. "He was a good man," she said, her voice quiet, almost wistful. "And he was a good son. He made his parents proud."

Cameron nodded.

"One afternoon at the racetrack, something went wrong coming out of a turn. His car clipped another and somehow went airborne, flipping several times before crashing and bursting into flames. His fire suit..." She shook her head. "There was nothing they could do. By the time they got the fire out enough to get him out of the car, he was gone and I wasn't even there. It was the most horrible day of my life."

Cameron held her close, but Summer was done with the tears.

"When I started falling for you," she said, "I thought God was playing a trick on me. Putting in my life yet another man who flirted with danger.

But I convinced myself that as fire chief, you were an administrator, someone who worked behind a desk doing paperwork, nothing dangerous like actually fighting fires."

"Oh, Summer."

"And then I found out that you go out on calls," she said, her voice a plaintive moan. "Instead of heading to safety, you run into burning buildings to save people, to be heroic. You and Garrett are like two sides of the same coin, but at least in Garrett's case, it was just the weekends when I had to fret and worry about him. With you, every single day you go to the fire station there's the potential that a blaze somewhere or some other emergency that has life-and-death consequences will be the one that kills you. That is just..." Summer shook her head. "It's just too much for me, Cameron."

She bowed her head and he knew that she had finally said her piece.

"Summer, I..."

"And then today, of all days," she interrupted. "That horrible fire I saw on the news. It was like God was saying, 'See, this is what I plan for you—endless heartache.'"

Cameron needed to know without any hesitancy or misunderstanding just what she was going through.

"Sweetheart, what do you mean by today of all days?"

She stared down at her hands for a long time,

then rubbed her bare ring finger. Cameron noticed the gesture and realized it was where her wedding ring and probably an engagement ring once circled her finger.

His chest suddenly felt as if an elephant were taking a nap on it. Today held some major significance for her. And if he were a betting man, he would lay down money that it had to something to do with Dr. Garrett Spencer.

"Summer?"

She cast pain-filled eyes up at him and he knew what she was going to say.

"It was two years ago today," she said, on barely a whisper. "I was coping fairly well. As well as could be expected. Just a little melancholy. Nothing like last year when Spring, Winter, Autumn and my mother all descended on my house in Macon because they knew I would be a mess."

Summer shook her head. "No, today I was doing okay with it, you know? I got up, prayed, read some Scripture."

"Which ones?"

She smiled.

"Garrett's favorite, which was Isaiah 40:31. 'They that wait on the Lord shall renew their strength. They shall mount up with wings like eagles, they shall run and not be weary, they shall walk and not faint.' He had it professionally printed, matted and framed with a photograph of a soaring bald eagle, and that hung in his office at home. That's one of the few things that I kept and brought with me to Cedar Springs. You may have seen it when you did the house inspection."

"In the room over the garage. I remember thinking how spectacular it was and admired that you were a woman who professed her faith with such a dynamic display."

"That's the one that I've always found inspiring and liberating, as well." She then glanced at him and gave a wry smile. "There were many, many moments after the accident when I knew God had simply forsaken me. I was mad at Garrett for putting himself in such danger. I was mad at God for taking Garrett. And I was angry with myself for a whole cadre of grievances both real and imagined. But—" she shrugged "—time is a great healer. I couldn't, of course, see that, believe it or even hope it in those dark days after the crash, but in time it didn't hurt so much. And then, well, then I moved home to Cedar Springs to start my life over, or at least I should say start a new chapter of my life."

"What did you do after reading the Bible this morning?"

"Oh, there was more," Summer told him. "I turned to Song of Solomon because I wanted to read about love."

Cameron's head snapped up. "What was that?"

She smiled. "You heard me. I was marveling at the newness of life and love and the time of singing—how that whole thing about a closed door and an open window was really true. I was actually patting myself on the back for being calm but not maudlin and reflective instead of weepy on the anniversary of Garrett's death. Since I didn't know what my emotional state might be, I wasn't on the schedule to work at Manna, so the day was mine."

She made a vague hand gesture in the air, encompassing the two of them. "This thing between us," she finally settled on, "I've just been…"

"Human and hurting?"

The edge of her mouth quirked up. "Yes, I suppose that does sum it up. So I gardened a bit today, flipped through a magazine and then turned on the television, bouncing around. Then I caught the end of the midday news. A big fire. Likely arson. Several fire companies called out. Two firefighters injured. The flames…" she said, shuddering, her voice again ragged and hurting. "The flames were shooting up like an inferno. And the news reporter at the scene never said who was injured, just that two local firefighters were rushed to the hospital. I didn't know if you were all right. And then I knew, I just knew, that you probably weren't. I called several times."

She burst into tears again. Cameron pulled her into his arms. He murmured soothing words to her. "I'm okay, Summer. I am right here, beside you. Safe and sound."

She hiccupped. "You have to remember that it was all like the time before. Like when you first showed up at my door with those two firefighters. All I saw was the uniform and it looked like…"

"I know, sweetheart. I know," Cameron said.

When she calmed, he held her hands and stared into her eyes.

"I am sorry, Summer, I am so very, very sorry that you had to go through that stress today. Yes, my job is dangerous. But I'm okay."

"Now," she wailed. "You're okay *now.* But what about next time?"

He was silent for a moment.

Lord, give me the words to explain to her what You've called me to do.

A split second later, a peace descended on Cameron and he knew what he needed to tell her and just how to do it.

"Summer, you know how you have those favorite Scriptures? Well, I have one, too. It is a verse that the Lord put on my heart when I was a teenager." He dug in his back pocket, pulled out a small card from his wallet and read to her:

"'When you pass through the waters, I will be with you; and when you pass through the rivers, they will not sweep over you. When you walk through the fire, you will not be burned; the flames will not set you ablaze. Do not be afraid, for I am with you.'

"Those words," Cameron said tucking the card back in his wallet, "that assurance… It seemed to speak to me on a lot of levels back then and I adopted it as my personal mantra. The promise that the Lord is with me every step of the way is an incredible comfort. I am well trained, Summer, and I make it my business to make sure that everyone who works for me or with me is equally well trained and prepared. I am a professional at what I do and I know that it is the calling that the Lord put on me."

"But you could die," Summer said.

"We're all going to die, honey."

"That isn't what I mean," she said. "It…it's just the thought that freaks me out. The thought of the fire, the flames. When Garrett died…" Summer shuddered as if taken by a chill, though the early evening air remained balmy.

He rubbed her arms, warming her. "Summer, I cannot promise you that I won't die while fighting a fire, but I can promise you that I will be careful."

Cameron knew that Summer Darling Spencer was in his life for a reason. Over the course of just a few short weeks, he had fallen in love with her—despite their different backgrounds, despite the differences in their class and wealth, and despite this newly revealed fear she harbored, he was absolutely, positively, head over heels in love with her.

Did that make him an impossible dreamer?

No, he thought. It made him a man who knew and trusted that the Lord would give him the partner He meant for him to have—the woman who would be his help mate, his equal and his wife in holy matrimony.

Here he was thinking about wedding rings and picket fences and Summer was struggling with an issue that could be a deal breaker.

I need some help here, Lord.

"The guys who were injured, the ones the TV reporter said were injured? How are they? Did they make it?" she asked.

He nodded. "Both of them are doing just fine," he said. "That's why I was delayed in finding you. When we left the scene, I went back to the station house to get cleaned up, then I went by your place."

"You did?"

"When I couldn't reach you by phone, either your cell or the landline at the house, I started worrying. I did a swing by Manna but they said you weren't on the schedule for a couple of days. I tried calling you again. And then I called Spring."

"Oh, dear."

He chortled. "Yeah, you could say that."

"So that's how you found me out here. I was wondering."

"Yep."

"She made me promise something that, at the time, didn't make much sense. I didn't understand," Cameron said.

"I guess you've already figured out that Spring is something of a protective bird when it comes to her little sisters."

"Loud and clear," Cameron said.

"So, what did she make you promise?"

"That I would be gentle with you."

A shadow of a smile creased her lips. "But she didn't tell you why."

It was not a question. She knew that her sister would not have betrayed a confidence, and in hindsight, Cameron could appreciate that. At the time, though, while he was going out of his mind with worry when he couldn't reach Summer, he thought Spring was just giving him a hard time because she wanted to give him grief.

Now he knew that Dr. Spring Darling wasn't being difficult. She was, in her own way, warning him that Summer was having a rough time of it because of the anniversary of her husband's death. Little did Cameron know that he had unintentionally added to Summer's angst and fear today. Her anxiety, well-placed, had prompted her to retreat to a place where she felt safe. Even if sitting on the top edge of an old silo did not rank up there with the most relaxing of spots for quiet contemplation.

"When Spring assured me you were all right, I went to the hospital. They were just finishing up with Jose Garcia who was being treated and released."

Summer gasped. "Jose? From Station One?"

Cameron nodded. "He's okay, Summer. Trust me. He's back at home now. The emergency room doc told me Jimmy Armstrong, the other injured man, is going to be okay, too, but they are keeping him overnight for observation. He had some smoke inhalation and some second-degree burns that they want to keep an eye on before letting him go home. But he's going to be fine."

Cameron grinned. "And knowing Jimmy, he is going to milk this for the next six months with the ladies. He's from Station Three, so I don't think you've met him. He's a good man."

"I'm glad the guys who were injured today are okay."

"Me, too," he said. "The investigation is going to take a while. There was evidence of arson."

"Who would do such a thing?"

Cameron shook his head. "I don't know. But that's what we're going to find out."

They fell silent for a moment, then, he said softly, "Summer?"

She cast inquisitive eyes at him.

"I'm glad you love me. I love you, too."

Her eyes filled with tears. "Don't cry," he said, gently thumbing away the moisture.

His gaze dipped to her mouth.

"Cameron?"

He answered her question by sealing his mouth to hers in a kiss filled with all the love and tenderness that he felt toward her.

Cameron was the first to, reluctantly, pull back.

"Summer, can we continue this on the ground?"

Chapter Twenty-One

The next day traffic was heavy in Durham, with people headed home from their jobs in the Research Triangle area. Cameron had asked her to accompany him to the lawyer's office. He'd already had one shock that day. The safe deposit box at Mickey Flynn's bank held important papers and bank books. The balances were staggering.

Mickey had lived a simple life. With no family to care for, he'd invested his income over the years. His investments had done well and he'd left it all, his house, his vehicles and his money, to Cameron.

"You all right?" Summer asked.

Cameron glanced over at her. "I'm not sure. We were close, but I had no idea."

"That he viewed you as the son he never had?"

Cameron nodded.

"You're a very wealthy man now."

"Why do I get the distinct impression that that amuses you?"

"Because it does," she said.

Cameron had taken off his suit jacket. It hung from a hook in the backseat and he'd unbuttoned his white shirt and rolled up the sleeves.

Summer was glad to see him at least look more relaxed than he obviously felt.

"Uh-huh," Cameron said, obviously distracted.

"Cam?"

He kept his eyes on the road. Summer's own gaze followed his, but didn't see anything amiss.

Summer glanced at him. "What's wrong?"

Cameron nodded with his head. "Look at that car. Up ahead on the left. The blue sedan to the left of the yellow cab. It's been weaving. They're gonna cause an…"

Before he could get the word *accident* out, the vehicle about five cars ahead of them that he'd been watching crashed into another then flipped over.

"Hold on!"

Cameron made several defensive turns to avoid hitting anyone or being hit.

Terrified, Summer braced one hand on the dashboard and clutched her seat belt strap with the other.

Cameron brought the car to an abrupt halt in the median. The sharp braking propelled Summer forward, but her hand was braced on the dashboard. Her heart was beating rapidly.

"You okay?"

"Uh-huh," she managed after a few stunned moments.

"Call 911," Cameron barked.

He was on his way out the door before Summer opened her eyes to discover they hadn't been hit.

She saw a blur as he popped the trunk, grabbed something and ran toward the accident scene.

Summer sat in her seat, shaking—trying to get a grip on what had just happened.

Accident.

Cameron had seen it coming.

Fire.

That's all she saw, all she registered. Flames shot from beneath the vehicle that had crashed, causing the accident. She clenched her eyes closed, imagining the body inside the burning car being engulfed in flames, the driver unable and incapable of doing anything except feeling a horrifying pain.

But it wasn't Garrett in that car. This was not the fiery crash that killed him.

It was Cameron.

Cameron, she thought in a panic.

He'd run *toward* the danger.

Lord, keep him safe, please.

Now the roadway was jammed with stalled cars. Several people rushed toward the accident scene. Some with cell phones held out like urban paparazzi, but others like Cameron blasting the flames with fire extinguishers they'd pulled from their own vehicles.

She saw him directing some of the other Good Samaritans toward the spots that would enable the passengers to be rescued.

In the distance, Summer heard the blare of emergency sirens. Already, help was on the way.

"Call 911."

He'd asked her to do one simple thing. But she hadn't managed to summon help. She hadn't dialed 911. She hadn't responded.

All she'd done was panic.

She lifted an unsteady hand to her face, still watching as Cameron handed off his fire extinguisher to another man then scrambled on the ground to... She leaned forward, trying to see what he was doing.

It looked like sawing.

Sawing?

The knife! He always had a Swiss Army knife with him. Suddenly what he was doing on the ground made sense. Cameron was cutting through the seat belt to free the driver.

Two other men helped another occupant of the vehicle to safety and away from the burning car that crashed.

Cameron remained alert, swinging into action when and where it was needed. With no consideration of his own safety, he moved to help others.

Peace, even in the midst of the horrific scene, enveloped her.

Fear had kept her bound, had momentarily paralyzed her. But God's love, His grace and His mercy would always be there, waiting for her to embrace the gifts of the Father. Those gifts were peace, comfort and an assurance that God was the one in control…of all things.

Even an accident on the road.

The Lord had sent a hero into her life. One who fought the Lord's battles on an uncommon ground.

"Thank you, Lord," she said again.

Summer smiled, even as she opened the passenger door and went to the trunk. She had teased him about his go bag and the storage box of supplies in his trunk. But they were there for a reason. Cameron had water and blankets and probably a heavy-duty first-aid kit and other things that might assist with accident victims. She grabbed the items and ran forward.

A man and a woman were tending to a nearly hysterical woman when Summer approached with bottles of water and twisted the cap on one of them.

"Here," she said as she sat on the ground beside the woman and took her hand. "Try to take a few sips."

"My mom! My mom's in there."

"They're getting her out," Summer said, surprised at her own calm given the situation. Indeed,

Cameron and two firefighters were pulling the driver to safety even as they watched.

Firefighters were on the run, hauling hoses to douse the remaining flames. Onlookers continued to record the unfolding drama with smartphones and tablets.

Cameron glanced up for a moment.

When he spotted Summer, his brows lifted in surprise. He mouthed, "I love you."

"Love you, too," she said back to him.

A moment later, Cameron was back in the fray, directing an EMT, doing what he'd been called to do.

Epilogue

When the second Sunday rolled around the following month, Cameron knew what to expect at Lovie Darling's house. He and Summer usually attended Sunday worship services together at The Fellowship, but on the second Sunday of the month they were at First Memorial Church of Cedar Springs in the pew he'd come to recognize was the Darling family's row.

He had a standing invitation to dinner at Lovie Darling's home and was looking forward to again sharing a meal with Summer's family.

Today brought two additional guests to the table, one of which surprised him.

The Reverend Doctor Joseph Graham, pastor of First Memorial, was already in Lovie Darling's cozy parlor when Summer and Cameron arrived.

"Ladies and gentleman," Cameron said, holding Summer's hand out as if in presentation. "May

I introduce you to the new volunteer coordinator at Manna."

Summer accepted congratulations from her family and pastor.

"So you'll be running the place now?" the Reverend Doctor Graham asked.

"Just the volunteer part and, of course, the meals. I told the board I wasn't qualified to head up a nonprofit, but that I did have coordinating skills that could be put to good use. They're going to search for a director who will be responsible for everything else."

"Congratulations, dear," Lovie said, giving Summer a hug.

The minister leaned in toward Cameron. "I see it takes a Darling to get you to First Memorial at least once a month," Doctor Graham said, teasing him.

"I enjoy the services you have," he said.

The minister chuckled and dipped his head toward Summer. "So you say."

"Reverend Graham, don't tease the boy," Lovie Darling said, walking her daughter back to Cameron. "He's a delightful dinner guest." She winked at Cameron.

The doorbell rang and Summer excused herself from both Cameron's embrace and the room to see to it. When she returned a few moments later, it was with Georgina Lundsford from the Historical Review Advisory Committee.

Spring joined them. "Oh, I'm so glad you're here,

Georgina. I want to show you what I found out about the firm that's…"

Georgina held a hand up to halt Spring. "I promised your mother that there would be no talk about that development deal," she announced.

Lovie Darling nodded. "That topic is off the table today since we want to enjoy our meal without indigestion."

"But…" Spring sputtered. "I have…"

"Not today," Lovie said.

"Come and get it," Autumn called from the doorway. "And hurry up before Winter tries to mess with one of my dishes."

Lovie, the minister, Georgina and Spring headed toward the dining room. Cameron held Summer back by hooking an arm around her waist and tugging her close to him.

"Hey, you," he said.

She turned in his arms and smiled at him. Cameron stole a quick kiss that lingered.

"You *really* don't want Winter fiddling with the food," Summer murmured against his mouth.

"Hmm," Cameron said as he reluctantly released her.

"Seriously, Cam. She's likely to add ketchup to the béarnaise sauce or to microwave a soufflé."

Cameron laughed, but said, "They'll be fine without us for a few minutes. There's something I wanted to talk to you about."

She cast searching blue eyes up at him. Cameron

led her to one of the loveseats in Lovie Darling's parlor, a room he'd come to associate with scrumptious hors d'oeuvres and family. With something of a Pavlovian response, he regarded this room as the place where good things—be they food or conversation—happened before the main course.

"What's going on with you?" Summer asked as he settled her on the cushion.

"There's something I want to ask you," he said.

"Okay. But dinner's getting cold."

Cameron chuckled. "Remind me to keep you fed from now on."

She cocked her head at a little angle. "Cameron?"

"Do you know how much I love you?" he asked.

Her eyes widened as he lowered himself to one bended knee before her.

"I think I fell in love with you the minute you fell into my arms earlier this summer. What I've come to discover as I've gotten to know you is that not only are you beautiful, you are loving and kind and funny and gorgeous and spirit-filled and did I mention beautiful?"

She smiled. "Cameron."

"Shh," he said. "Let me finish. I only plan to do this once in my life."

She grinned at him and then waved at him to continue.

"You have made me a better man," Cameron said. "I'm not perfect. Not by a long shot. And you know I still need some, er, work, shall we say, in a few areas. But I know that with you at my side, I can be an even better man."

He tucked his hand in his suit jacket pocket and pulled out a small dark velvet box.

Thumbing it open, he turned it to her where a diamond in an antique filigree setting sparkled. "This was my grandmother's," he said. "She and my grandfather were married for sixty-nine years. He died in his sleep the evening before their seventieth wedding anniversary. She was perfectly healthy but died less than a week later of what the doctors said was simply a broken heart."

He groaned. "I'm making a mess of this," he said. "Here I am trying to propose and I'm talking about people dying."

"You're doing a pretty good job, I think," Summer said.

His gaze met hers and there was hope and love shining in his eyes.

"The ring is old," he said. "And old-fashioned. If you don't like it, we can get the diamond put in a new setting or design one together."

He took the ring out of the box and set the box on the floor. "Summer Darling Spencer, would you do me the honor and the privilege of becoming my bride?"

Tears that had already filled Summer's eyes flowed freely. She laughed as she wiped them away.

"What is it?" Cameron asked.

"I'm glad I used the waterproof mascara today."

That earned her a chuckle from him and then Cameron was all serious and intent again. He took her left hand in his and held the ring in his other.

"Will you marry me, Summer?"

She nodded.

Then, she said, "Yes, yes, yes!"

From across the room came applause and a sharp whistle that could only have come from Coach Autumn.

Unaware of their audience, Summer and Cameron turned to see Lovie, Autumn, Winter and Spring Darling as well as their dinner guests grinning and applauding in the open French doorway of the parlor.

"It's about time," Autumn said to the couple. Then to the others: "They're engaged now. Can we eat?"

"You don't have a romantic bone in your body," Winter accused her little sister.

"Yes, she does," Spring declared. "A month ago she was whining about wanting to plan a wedding. Now she'll get to actually do it."

Autumn rolled her eyes and just shook her head, but she looked as pleased as her sisters and her mother.

Lovie Darling was dabbing her eyes with a small lace-edged hankie.

Grinning, Cameron turned back to Summer.

"I know summer is your favorite season," he said. "Would you like a summer wedding?

She shook her head. "No, Cam. A year is too long to wait to be your bride. I don't need or want a big to-do. Unless you do," she quickly added.

He grinned and looked over his shoulder. "Put that planning on a fast track, Autumn." Then, with his attention back on Summer, he added for her ears only. "I'd haul you off to a justice of the peace right now if I could."

Summer's delight showed in the sparkle in her eyes.

He slipped the ring on her fourth finger. It was a bit loose on her slender hand.

"We'll get that sized," he said. "And changed to a new setting, one that you like."

"Sized, yes," Summer said. "But other than that, it's perfect. I'm a traditional kind of girl, remember? There's a lot of love and tradition here. And it would be an honor for me to wear your grandmother's ring. I like it just the way it is."

"I love you, Summer Spencer."

"And I you, Chief Cam. You're my very own firefighter hero."

* * * * *

Dear Reader,

What a delight to again share with you a novel of faith and love. My first Love Inspired novels were set in the fictional town of Wayside, Oregon. This time, I am writing about a place a little closer to home: North Carolina.

Cedar Springs, North Carolina, is not a real place. My hope, however, is that Cedar Springs and its residents will feel as real to you as the people you interact with on a daily basis.

The idea for Common Ground and its three congregations came from a photograph of three ministers of diverse ages that appeared in the local newspaper. I kept staring at it and wondered why it resonated so much with me. The four Darling sisters have been with me for many years, just waiting for the right time to tell their stories. The confluence of the photograph in the newspaper and the characters I had in mind merged and a story was born. Before I knew it, Faith in Cedar Springs became a reality.

Thank you for joining me in the first of what I hope will be a long journey exploring the lives, loves, conflicts and struggles of the men and women who belong to, are aided by or are impacted by the three Common Ground congregations—the First Memorial Church of Cedar Springs, The Fellowship, and the Chapel of the Groves—as they find Faith in Cedar Springs.

Praying for your blessings and God's mercy.
Felicia Mason

Questions for Discussion

1. Summer Spencer found love despite her fears. What personal lessons did you learn from her struggle to open up and let herself love Cameron?

2. Were Summer's fears justified? What about Cameron's insecurities about their different economic positions? How can class and economic differences either derail or enhance relationships?

3. What are the central themes of the novel? How are they illustrated throughout the book?

4. The Common Ground ministries are geared to provide ministry opportunities for members of the three diverse congregations in Cedar Springs: First Memorial, The Fellowship and the Chapel of the Groves. Does your church or congregation offer community outreach opportunities and ministries? If so, which are the most effective?

5. Grief is expressed in a number of ways in the novel, as is the notion of rebirth. Identify and reflect on some of them.

6. Which secondary characters would you most like to see in a story of his or her own?

7. Summer Spencer and her sisters resemble each other physically, but are very different in other respects. How do you and your siblings or close family members differ? How are you the same?

8. Cameron was open in professing his faith and connecting his work in fire service with his witness for Christ. How do you profess the Gospel and Christ through your own job, hobbies or service?

9. The death of Mickey Flynn hit Cameron hard. What mentors in your own life do you cherish? Which have you lost and how did that loss affect you?

10. In the book, the primary ministry at Manna at Common Ground is feeding the poor, the homeless and those who are unable to get a nourishing meal. What services are offered in your community for those populations? Have you ever considered volunteering to assist one of them? Why or why not?

LARGER-PRINT BOOKS!

GET 2 FREE
LARGER-PRINT NOVELS
PLUS 2 FREE
MYSTERY GIFTS

Love Inspired
SUSPENSE
RIVETING INSPIRATIONAL ROMANCE

Larger-print novels are now available...